"What's going on?"

Hazel demanded an explanation for his evacuation order. "I know there's no fire. I heard the dispatcher say she was sending a unit. Who's coming?"

"The bomb squad," Burke answered.

"A bomb? I thought it was just another... I hadn't gotten a letter this week. I'd hoped Aaron would stop once his parole officer spoke with him. You think he sent a bomb to my clinic?"

"Gunny alerted there was an explosive. His nose is never wrong. I need you outside, too. Gunny and I have to clear the building."

"But...that's what the bomb squad is for, right? Shouldn't you have backup?"

"Go. It's what we do." He reached out to cup her cheek in his hand. "But I need you to be safe before I can go to work."

She nodded. Then she reached up and covered his hand with hers. "I'll see you outside," she vowed, as if her will could guarantee that they'd be reunited.

K-9 PROTECTOR

USA TODAY Bestselling Author
JULIE MILLER

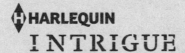
HARLEQUIN
INTRIGUE

For Dr. Missy and the staff at Animal Medical Clinic in
Grand Island, NE.

You've taken such good care of many of our pets. And you've
supported us when we've lost our furry loved ones. Thank you.

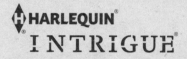

ISBN-13: 978-1-335-13667-1

K-9 Protector

Recycling programs
for this product may
not exist in your area.

Harlequin Enterprises ULC
22 Adelaide St. West, 40th Floor
Toronto, Ontario M5H 4E3, Canada
www.Harlequin.com

Printed in U.S.A.

Julie Miller is an award-winning *USA TODAY* bestselling author of breathtaking romantic suspense—with a National Readers' Choice Award and a Daphne du Maurier Award, among other prizes. She has also earned an *RT Book Reviews* Career Achievement Award. For a complete list of her books, monthly newsletter and more, go to juliemiller.org.

Books by Julie Miller

Harlequin Intrigue

Rescued by the Marine
Do-or-Die Bridesmaid
Personal Protection
Target on Her Back
K-9 Protector

The Precinct

Beauty and the Badge
Takedown
KCPD Protector
Crossfire Christmas
Military Grade Mistletoe
Kansas City Cop

The Precinct: Bachelors in Blue

APB: Baby
Kansas City Countdown
Necessary Action
Protection Detail

The Precinct: Cold Case

Kansas City Cover-Up
Kansas City Secrets
Kansas City Confessions

Visit the Author Profile page at Harlequin.com.

CAST OF CHARACTERS

Sgt. Jedediah Burke—Commander of the K-9 division at KCPD. He trains dogs and handlers, leads men and commands respect. When the woman he's secretly loved for years is threatened, Burke puts all his skills, his K-9 partner and his heart on the line to keep her safe.

Dr. Hazel Cooper—Veterinarian who oversees the care for KCPD's canine officers. A harrowing divorce has made her leery of trusting any man with her heart again. But when a stalker delivers bomb parts and threatens to blow up everything she loves, she turns to her friend Burke for help. She trusts that Burke will protect her. But can she trust that their love is the real thing?

Gunny—Burke's K-9 partner. A Czech German shepherd dog who sniffs out explosives and protects his handler—and his favorite veterinarian—from any threat.

Ashley and Polly Cooper—Hazel's grown daughters think it's time for Mom to pursue a relationship again.

Aaron Cooper—Hazel's ex-husband is out of prison.

Todd Mizner—Vet tech at Hazel's animal medical clinic.

Wade Hanson—A client whose dangerously ill dog needs Hazel's help.

Shannon Bennett—Burke's ex-wife.

Joe Sciarra—Ashley's new boyfriend.

Chapter One

"He was totally flirting with you, Mom."

Dr. Hazel Cooper startled as her older daughter opened the door to the examination room. She crumpled the disturbing note she'd been reading in her fist and stuffed it into the pocket of her scrubs jacket before fixing a smile on her face and turning around. "You mean Sergeant Burke? I was up to my elbows in dead ear mites and cleaning goop. He brought Gunny in so I could clean his ears and make sure the medication is clearing up the yeast infection he had. He helped me hold the dog and we discussed updating Gunny's leptospirosis vaccine. None of that is flirting."

Ashley Cooper pulled on a pair of sterile gloves before sweeping the pile of soiled gauze and cotton swabs off the stainless steel table into the trash. "I was here to hold the dog. Burke didn't have to."

"Gunny is his boy. Burke is a hands-on kind of owner."

"I can tell he's *hands-on*," Ashley teased. "When

Burke moved around the table, he brushed against you. By the way, *you* didn't move away."

Hazel shook her head at that silly reasoning. "Practicality. Not evidence. I wanted to show him that the infection had cleared up."

"Methinks she doth protest too much." Ashley pulled aside the blinds on the exam room's window, giving Hazel a clear view of the parking lot and the man in the black KCPD uniform loading his Czech shepherd, Gunny, into the back of his K-9 unit truck. "He's a bachelor, right? I bet all kinds of women are throwing themselves at him. And yet he brings his dog here to trade quips and rub shoulders with you."

Jedediah Burke opened the back door and issued a sharp command, and the black-and-tan brindle dog, built like a sturdier German shepherd, jumped inside. The muscular dog was strong and moved his powerful body with a fluid grace. Not unlike his partner and handler. As commander of KCPD's K-9 unit, Burke oversaw the ongoing training of the twelve dogs and handlers working for the department, in addition to his own duties as a patrol officer. The material of Burke's fitted black T-shirt stretched tautly across his broad shoulders and tapered down to the thick leather utility belt at his waist and the gun holstered to the thigh of his black cargo pants.

She tamped down the little frissons of awareness that hummed inside her blood as Burke leaned into the truck, pulling other parts of his uniform taut across another well-defined part of his body. The man was fit and interesting and aging like a fine wine. And she really did appreciate a good merlot.

Hazel shook her head at the analogy that sprang to mind. Her daughter's fantasies must be rubbing off on her. She pulled the curtain and turned away from the window. Yes, Jedediah Burke was an attractive man, but she wasn't in the market for romance. Or whatever sort of relationship her daughter was imagining for her.

She'd done just fine without a man for sixteen years.

Many of those years had been difficult. All of them had been lonely. But after that blindingly stellar mistake she'd made in saying "I do" to her ex-husband, could she really trust herself to handle anything more than a few frissons of sexual awareness? Could she ever know a man well enough to give in to her hormones and risk her heart again?

"He's not a bachelor," Hazel corrected, needing to inject some logic and common sense into this conversation. "Burke is divorced." She disposed of the syringe in the sharps container and peeled off her gloves.

"What a coincidence. So are you." Ashley held up the trash can for Hazel to toss her gloves. "You have that in common. I bet that gives you plenty to talk about besides vet care and police work. Failed marriages. Broken hearts. Have you ever comforted each other? I bet he's good in the sack, too."

"Ashley Marie Cooper! I am not just your mother—I'm your boss." She glanced toward the door, confirming it was closed and that no one was overhearing this mother-daughter conversation. "You will not be discussing me being in the sack with anyone. Especially here at work, where another employee could overhear."

"Did I mention you specifically?" she teased. "Or have you been thinking the same thing?"

"Give it a rest." Hazel pulled up the computer screen on the workstation beside the sink to update Gunny's records. "Sergeant Burke doesn't flirt. And neither do I."

Ashley was messing with the curtains again. "Then why is he coming back in here?"

"What?" Hazel spun around to look through the window. Burke was striding across the parking lot, jogging up the concrete steps to the clinic's front door.

"Got you. You just fluffed your hair."

Hazel pulled her fingers down to her side. "My bangs were in my eyes."

Ashley touched her mouth. "A little lip gloss wouldn't hurt, either. You should keep a tube in your pocket." She reached into the pocket of her own scrubs and pulled out a small compact of pink raspberry balm. "Here. Borrow mine."

Hazel backed away from the offer. "You should find a nice young man your own age and focus on him instead of creating a love life for me." She turned her attention back to the computer. "Burke and I work together. He runs KCPD's K-9 unit, and I manage the dogs' health concerns. We're friends. Colleagues. Period."

Ashley pulled the disinfectant spray from the cabinet beside Hazel and spritzed the examination table. "Then you are woefully out of practice in reading men. He was eyeing your butt when you bent over to pick up the cotton swab you dropped. When was the last time you went out on a date?"

"Why are we having this conversation?"

"Because you were just looking at his butt, too. Or is it the square jaw or those deep brown eyes you like?"

"Why are you sizing up Jedediah Burke's attributes? He's old enough to be your father."

"He's not old enough to be yours." Ashley came up beside Hazel and draped her arm around her shoulders. "Besides, hot is hot at any age."

Although Hazel absolutely loved having Ashley working with her at the clinic as a vet tech, they were going to have to set some ground rules about conversations getting too personal here at work. Especially around the rest of the staff, who might not be familiar with her daughters Ashley and Polly's lifelong quest to play matchmaker for their single mother ever since she divorced their father after he went to prison to serve a fifteen-year sentence.

Ashley and Polly had been children then, ages six and four. If only they knew the whole reason for that divorce—and why an eight-year sentence had been extended to fifteen. They'd already been traumatized enough, and Hazel had done everything in her power to protect them. There were some secrets that no child needed to know about her father.

Hazel turned and pressed a kiss to Ashley's cheek. "Just for that remark, you get to finish cleaning up in here. I believe Mrs. Stinson's corgis are waiting for me in room one."

"That's not all that's waiting out there."

A soft knock at the exam room door mercifully ended the conversation. Before Hazel could reach it, the door swung open and Jedediah Burke filled the door frame.

"Hey, Dr. Coop." His low-pitched drawl skittered across her eardrums and made various nerve endings prick to attention throughout her body. He removed his black KCPD ball cap in a politely deferential gesture that spoke to long-ignored feminine appreciations inside her. "One of your receptionists out front said you were still back here. That it was all right to come in."

Good grief, Ashley was right. He did have a square jaw, dusted by an intriguing mix of dark brown stubble salted with silver, which echoed the military-short cut that framed his handsome face.

Why had Ashley put these thoughts in her head? Not that a normal, healthy woman of any age wouldn't notice that Jedediah Burke was an attractive man. But she'd never allowed herself to react to the masculinity oozing from every pore and that air of natural authority he carried on those broad shoulders. And now she was…reacting. Former Army sergeant turned veteran KCPD cop Jedediah Burke was…Burke. A longtime acquaintance. A colleague. A friend.

He wasn't potential dating material any more than

the author of those sickly personal letters she'd been receiving was.

Remembering the disturbing notes effectively put the kibosh on these uncomfortable feelings that had surfaced, allowing her to once again bury her attraction to Burke under a friendly facade. "That's fine." She could even get past the staring and offer him a genuine smile. "Did you forget something?"

"Two things. I think I left Gunny's chew toy in the exam room. That dog is all about play. If I lose his favorite toy, he won't work for me."

Ashley picked it up from beneath a chair and handed it to him. "Here."

"Thanks." He smiled and nodded before turning those whiskey-brown eyes back to Hazel. "Plus, I forgot to tell you that I'll be in training sessions with a couple of new recruits all morning tomorrow. The rest of my team and their dogs are coming in to have lunch before you run the monthly checkups on the canine crew. Ed's Barbecue is catering the meal as a thank-you for Pike Taylor and K-9 Hans stopping those teenagers who tried to rob him last month. You're welcome to join us."

"Ed's Barbecue?" She didn't need to fake her enthusiasm at the mention of her favorite hole-in-the-wall barbecue joint. "Are you getting the scalloped barbecue potatoes?"

Burke grinned. "Can't have the pulled pork without the potatoes."

"I can't pass those up." She'd walk an extra mile to keep the carbs from settling on her already round hips for a chance to indulge in Ed's creamy, yummy potato dish. "I'll get there are soon as I can tomorrow. Make sure you save me some."

"Will do. See you tomorrow." He put his hat back on and tipped the brim of it to her and then to Ashley. "Dr. Coop. Ash."

"Burke." Ashley's squee of excitement burst from her lips the moment the door closed behind him. She threw her arms around Hazel and hugged her. "See? That's flirting. He asked you out to lunch."

"Down, girl." Hazel patted her daughter's arm before pulling away. "The men and women on his team and all their dogs will be there, too. Nothing says romance like routine checkups on slobbery canines and updating vaccinations."

Ashley rolled her green eyes toward the ceiling in a dramatic gesture. "You're killin' me here, Mom. Burke's a stud. And a nice guy. You two share interests and don't have any trouble communicating with each other. Isn't that what you want in a relationship?" Hazel returned to the computer to finish her updates. Ashley followed, her tone sounding more mature, less giddy. "You are an attractive, intelligent, funny, desirable woman who shouldn't be alone as much as you are. Dad hasn't been a part of our lives for sixteen years now. Yes, he's been out of prison for a few months—but we've made it abundantly clear that we don't need his kind of trouble in our lives anymore. Polly and I are grown-up now. You don't have to be the stalwart single mom who provides for us and protects us 24-7. It's okay to move on and fall in love again." She shrugged as though any kind of protest would be a nonstarter. "Polly and I agree— Jedediah Burke is a prime candidate for you to date. Or have a fling with."

"You dragged your sister into discussing my love life?" Two years younger than Ashley, and a junior in nursing at Saint Luke's, Polly Cooper might be the quieter of her two daughters, but there was no denying that she could be just as stubborn about a cause as the outgoing Ashley. "Of course you have." With a weary sigh, she faced the younger version of herself. "First of all, I'm your mother and I love you both, and I will never *not* want to protect you in any way I can. Secondly, I know it's in good fun, but this matchmaking has to stop. If Burke gets wind of this conversation, it might embarrass him. Not to mention embarrass me if anyone else overhears this grand design you have for us."

There was another soft knock at the door, and for a split second Hazel held her breath, half expecting, perhaps half hoping, that Burke had come back for some reason.

Instead, Todd Mizner, another of the three vet techs who worked for her, stepped into the room, reminding her of just how busy the clinic could get this time of the afternoon. Todd was a few years older than Ashley and was attractive in a nerdy-professor kind of way, with his dark-rimmed glasses and long-ish hair that he pulled back into a ponytail. The young man was driven to achieve, commuting twice a week to Manhattan, Kansas, to pursue his DVM degree while holding down this job, and he had a real knack for handling animals. Her daughter could do worse than a hardworking cutie like Todd.

Hazel turned to give Ashley a meaningful glance. "Speaking of grand designs…"

But her daughter shook her blond ponytail down her back, dismissing the matchmaking role reversal, and left the room.

Right. Much to Hazel's chagrin, Todd Mizner wasn't bad boy enough to suit Ashley's adventurous taste in men. Although Ashley had thankfully left her wild-child teenage years behind her, it was another lingering by-product in how the Cooper women dealt with the rest of the world after those long years of uncertainty surrounding Aaron Cooper's betrayal and the subsequent divorce, trial and incarceration.

"It's not so comfortable when the shoe's on the other foot, is it?" she called after Ashley before the door closed.

Todd joined Hazel at the counter while she printed off the notes for Gunny's file. "What was that about?"

"Nothing. Some girl talk."

He reached around her to click the computer mouse. "I've got the X-rays ready on that poodle with the herniated disk. Looks like there is a fracture in the pelvis."

"Oh, damn." That could mean surgery instead of the laser therapy she'd been planning on using to reduce the inflammation making the dog drag its right hind leg. She took her reading glasses from her chest pocket and waited for him to pull the film up on the screen.

Todd muttered a curse against her ear, reminding Hazel that he was standing right behind her. "This computer is doing its own thing again. I can't get the pictures I took to load."

Whether it was a problem with the software or the compatibility of the hardware, Hazel didn't know. And with patients waiting, she didn't have time to figure it out, either. "All right. I'll go look at the film in the X-ray room. You go on to exam three and sit with Maggie's owner. I know she's stressing about the accident. Make sure there's a box of tissues in the room and see if you can pull up the X-rays on the computer screen in there. I'll want to show her pictures to explain what's going on."

"Can't Ashley do that?"

"She's doing the prelim intake on Cassie and Reggie." Mrs. Stinson's corgis would have to wait until Hazel assessed the poodle's injuries and started treatment. "With the dog's age, Mrs. Miller may be thinking there's nothing we can do for Maggie. I don't want her alone in there." She tipped her chin up to Todd and smiled. "Go use some of that Mizner charm on her to keep her distracted until I can get there."

"But you promised I could scrub in on the next surgery. I want to be a part of the process from initial consult to seeing that dog walk again. Or fitting her for a wheelchair if therapy and surgery don't work."

Todd hadn't budged an inch from behind her, and when Hazel inhaled, her shoulder brushed against his chest. Squashing down an instant imprint of *eeuw* at the contact, Hazel stepped to the side, so she had room to turn and face him. She hadn't batted an eye when, as Ashley had pointed out, Burke had bumped into her. But even this accidental contact with the younger man felt somehow inappropriate. Maybe it was the stress of the long day. Or that awkward conversation with Ashley. Or maybe it was something else entirely that made her anxious to get on with her work. "We'll discuss it later. The priority is the patient's care right now—and that includes the owner as well as the pet."

"The more experience I get, the better. One of these days soon, I'll be finishing my classwork and interning…" Todd rested his hand on the counter beside her, his arm nearly circling around her as he winked. "Then you and I can be full partners."

The message in that letter burned through her pocket and seared her skin. *That* was what bothered her about Todd's tendency to be overly familiar with her. She gently pushed Todd back a step. "Personal space, Todd. We've had this discussion, remember?"

Maybe not such a great catch for her daughter, after all. Todd might be good with animals, but his people skills could use a little work.

He stepped back even farther, putting his hands up in mock surrender. "I don't mean anything by it, Dr. Coop. You know I'm harmless. You're jumpy today for some reason."

No. He was behaving in a way that she didn't appreciate. Not as a boss with her employee. Not as a woman with a man young enough to be her son. Not as someone who'd been receiving anonymous letters that spoke to a disturbing desire for a relationship. She pointed to the door, reminding him that she was the boss here. She didn't have to explain anything to a vet tech who worked for her. "Exam room three."

"Yes, ma'am. Whatever you need." While Todd headed across the lobby to the exam room on the opposite side, Hazel pushed through the swinging door leading into the restricted area where she performed surgery, stored meds and housed specialized equipment. She went straight to the X-ray room to see how poor little Maggie had fared after her fall down a flight of steps.

What she needed was time alone in the darkened room to clear her head. She pulled her glasses from her pocket to study the film. But the moment they touched the bridge of her nose, she thought of the letter and tugged them right back off.

She didn't need to pull out the letter to read it again. She knew every word by heart.

I've been watching you, Hazel.

Your bright green eyes are so intelligent, so pretty. Even when you wear your reading glasses, they shine and entice me. No man deserves you.

I want to be a part of your life. I want us to share everything.

I want you.

I want you.

I want you.

Hazel might not recognize flirting anymore—or

maybe she subconsciously chose to ignore it. Her relationship skills might be rusty since her divorce and bankruptcy and the threats and humiliation that had filled her life during her husband Aaron's trial and for several years afterward.

But she'd been a different person then. Now she knew when something wasn't right. A man who wrote *I want you* a dozen times on a letter, and then refused to sign it or even include a return address, did not have her best interests at heart.

This letter, and eight more she had like it at home, told her she'd become someone's obsession.

The feeling of being watched, of being stalked, of feeling terrorized in the places she was supposed to feel safe felt a lot like…

She gasped at the knock outside the open door. "Todd, I said…"

"Whoa." Jedediah Burke filled her doorway again. His hands raised in apology did nothing to lessen the impact of his size dwarfing the tiny room. "Sorry about that. You were really concentrating. Everything okay?"

When Hazel realized she was clutching her hand over her racing heart, she immediately reached for her glasses again and put them on. With his eyes narrowed on her, she doubted she was fooling him. He'd startled her, and he knew it. Avoiding Burke's probing gaze, she studied the troubling results of the X-ray. "You can't seem to leave."

After a moment he nodded. "I forgot to tell you what time lunch was tomorrow. I know I could have texted, but I was already here." He stepped into the room, stopping beside her chair to glance at the X-ray. Unlike when Todd had invaded her personal space, she knew the strongest urge to turn and lean into him—especially when his hand settled gently on her shoulder. "Did something happen? Lose a patient?"

Damn it. The man smelled good, too. An enticing combination of spicy soap and the subtle musk of the early-October afternoon clinging to his skin that only intensified in the small confines of the X-ray room.

Hazel considered brushing off his concern and sending him on his way. Then her peripheral gaze landed on the brass KCPD badge clipped onto his belt. Burke represented help and safety in more ways than one. She'd known him for five years now. She could trust him with this. She tucked her glasses back into her jacket pocket and tilted her gaze up to his. "Could I ask you something? As a police officer?"

"Of course." He pulled away, the moment of compassion masked by his wary alertness.

She pulled the note from her pocket and spared a few moments to smooth it open against the tabletop before handing it to him. "Would you read this?" He'd probably think she was being paranoid. Or maybe he'd be angry that she hadn't reported the letters sooner. His chiseled expression grew grimmer with every line he skimmed.

"Is that normal?" she asked.

"Who's it from?"

She hesitated a beat before answering. "I don't know."

"Then no, it's not." He leaned against the door frame, facing her again. "Got a jilted boyfriend I need to worry about?"

The friend she knew might be teasing her to help her feel a little less worried, but the cop was waiting for an answer.

She'd asked for his opinion. She owed it to him to give him a clearer understanding as to why an innocuous note could rattle her this much. "At first, I thought my ex-husband, Aaron, was writing me again. You probably remember him from the news a few years back." Burke nodded but waited for her to continue. "He used to send me flowery garbage like that when we were dating. I told him I wasn't impressed, and he stopped. He always said he liked my directness— until he went to trial. Then he wasn't real keen on me telling the truth. The letters he used to write from prison were straight-out blame for testifying against him. Those were angry tirades. I stopped opening his mail and then had a judge stop them altogether. I asked him not to have any contact with me or the girls. There were too many threats back when the trial…back when Aaron was arrested. He ruined a lot of lives when he raided those retirement funds. I didn't need his vile messages on top of the threats we were getting from other victims."

"*Other* victims?" Oh, hell. He'd picked up on that rare slip of the tongue. "Were you a victim, too?"

She shook her head instead of answering the question. "I just meant I thought the obsessive language meant they were from my ex."

"You said *they*?" Burke repeated, holding up the letter. "You thought *they* were from your ex."

Damn. He didn't miss a trick. No sense avoiding the full truth with this veteran cop. "That's the ninth one I've gotten since the first one came on my birthday, August 5."

"Nine letters in nine weeks?"

"The first ones were pretty innocuous. But…he seems to get angrier or more frustrated with each letter."

Burke turned the paper over, inspecting it for identifying clues she knew he wouldn't find. "Did the envelope have a post office stamp?"

"Kansas City. But no return address."

"Is Aaron still in prison?"

Hazel shook her head. "He got out on parole the end of last year. The restraining order should prevent him from having contact with me or the girls. But then these started arriving. They're not exactly a threat, but they're…unsettling."

"Do you know where he is now?"

She stood when he handed back the letter. "Our lives have been a lot more peaceful without him. I didn't want to jinx anything by reaching out to him. Even through a third party."

"I'll look into it." Burke reached for her hand. But it wasn't a reassuring squeeze he offered so much as a warning. "But I'm guessing he's here in Kansas City."

Chapter Two

"Uh…huh…" Hazel drew out her response as she looked through her scope into Gunny's ear. "Everything's looking pink and perfect. No signs of the infection."

Burke mirrored her, scooting around to the other side of the examination table while she moved to inspect Gunny's other ear. Although he trusted that Gunny would maintain his stay command until he released him, Burke had volunteered to hold the big dog while Hazel gave the Czech shepherd a final all clear on his ear treatments. With all the exam rooms full and clients waiting in the lobby, it was clear that Friday afternoon at the clinic was a busy time for boarding drop-offs and medical appointments. Letting Burke stay here to help not only freed up a member of her staff to work with another patient but also gave him a few minutes of privacy he needed to update Hazel on what he'd found out about her ex-husband and the letters.

There was one particularly disturbing item he'd discovered in Aaron Cooper's arrest record. While the cop in him wanted to dig into the details, the man in him wasn't sure how he'd handle what he might find. Besides, Hazel was a private person, and if she had chosen not to mention the incident in the five years they'd known each other, then he wasn't going to bring it up. Not yet, anyway. He understood about divorce and betrayal, and that the injured party did whatever she or he had to in order to move on with their lives.

But if push came to shove and there really was a credible threat here, or he had any inclination that history was going to repeat itself, then privacy be damned. He'd demand the whole truth from Hazel in order to mount the comprehensive security detail she might require. And if she still wouldn't share, he knew other ways to get the specifics he needed. But he wouldn't like going behind her back, and neither would she.

Burke scrubbed a hand over Gunny's brown-and-black head, more to keep the dog from falling asleep than to prevent him from acting up while he lay on the table and let Hazel check him out. His nostrils flared with a calming breath as he edited any emotion from his tone. She'd asked him to do this favor as a professional, not as the man who was finding it harder every day to respect the boundaries she put up between them. "I talked to Aaron's parole officer and notified Officer Kranitz about the letters. He'll ask your ex about them. If Kranitz thinks Aaron is responsible for sending them, he'll remind him about the restraining order. After that, another letter arrives and he's back in jail."

Hazel peered into the scope and nodded. "That can't prevent him from giving the letters to someone else to mail for him. Even at the worst of the lawsuits and legal proceedings, he always managed to have a couple of pals who seemed willing to do his bidding. Still don't know if he paid them to be his allies or relied on his rather convincing charm. One thing Aaron always excelled at was making deals."

Damn. Not one blink to reveal just what her ex-husband had been capable of, and what she must have gone through at his hand. Instead, she straightened and smiled up at him. "This ear is looking great, too. I'd say your partner is fit for duty."

No details today. Burke wasn't going to push, because he had a feeling Hazel would retreat to that unspoken distance between them that he'd worked patiently to overcome. He didn't want any of the closeness they'd settled into in this relationship, which was something more than friendship, yet something less than what he truly wanted, to erode.

"Good." He moved his hand along Gunny's fur to pet his flank as Hazel took over scratching around the dog's ears. He grinned at the way Gunny turned his head into her palm, savoring her touch. He ignored the sucker punch of jealousy he felt and ordered the dog up to a sit. "You're gettin' soft, big guy. I need to get you back to more than just training sessions."

Hazel set the scope on the counter behind her and came back to rub her hands around Gunny's jowls.

"Don't you listen to the mean ol' sergeant," she teased. "You're as tough as any cop on the force."

"Don't encourage him," Burke teased right back. "He's already got a big ego I have to keep in check."

Now the examination was done, and they were standing around spoiling his working K-9 instead of all three of them getting back to work. If Hazel hadn't shown him those creepy letters she'd been receiving and asked him to help her reclaim some peace of mind by finding out where they were coming from, he'd have no reason to be here at all.

While he couldn't say for certain who was sending her the anonymous notes, he had done everything he could to give her that peace of mind. "Your building downtown seems secure with the parking gate and coded entry system. While I don't like that wall of windows at the front of your condo where anybody and his brother could look in on you if they're in a high enough location, at least you're not on the ground floor. Plus, they've done a good job installing locks on the front door and fire escape windows."

"A refurbished historic building has structural limitations. I saved long and hard to buy that place. Plus, it's only a few blocks' drive from the clinic. At least it's in a good neighborhood near the library, hotels and convention center."

Burke nodded. No place was truly safe if someone was determined to get to her. And the fact that the perp had said he was watching her made him think he knew exactly where she lived. Or worked. Or both. "I also talked to hospital police regarding

Polly and the potential threats. They'll do what they can to keep an eye on things there. Polly and Ashley's apartment has good security, too." His fingers stilled in Gunny's fur beside the KCPD vest the dog wore. "I've also got Aaron's current address. If the harassment doesn't stop and you want Gunny and me to pay him a personal visit, I will."

Her hands stilled as well, and her cheeks went pale. "I hope it doesn't come to that. You've been very thorough."

"How else would I do my job?"

Hazel reached across the dog to squeeze his forearm. Every nerve ending in his body zeroed in on the skin-on-skin caress. "Thank you."

"You're welcome."

He was tall enough that he could lean across the table and kiss her if he wanted. And damn, he wanted to. He wanted to ask her out, too, as evidenced by that half-assed attempt to invite her to lunch last week. There was something about Hazel Cooper that made him stupid like a teenager again. Probably because he hadn't wanted a woman the way he wanted her for a long time. She made him laugh. She got his dry humor. She was a smart woman and damn good at her job, and, despite trying to camouflage them in those scrubs and jeans, she had just about the sweetest curves he'd ever seen. And though he suspected that tomboyish pixie cut of hair was all about convenience, the silvery blond bangs drew his attention to her pretty green eyes, and the short length highlighted the elegant column of her neck—a whole stretch of creamy skin he'd like to nuzzle his lips against and taste with his tongue.

But he respected her unspoken wish to keep a friendly professional relationship between them. Besides, his ex-wife, Shannon, had burned him badly enough that he'd choose a woman whose friendship and loyalty he could trust without question over satisfying any itch he had to find out what Hazel's skin tasted like. Pity he couldn't find a friendship like this and a lover in the same woman. He might not be such a crusty, out-of-practice horndog around Dr. Coop if that was the case.

It took a slurp of Gunny's tongue across Hazel's jaw to break the standing-and-staring spell that had possessed him for a few seconds. Burke wisely shrugged off her touch and pulled away as she laughed. "Sorry about that. I guess he's done. Gunny, down. Good boy."

He petted Gunny's flanks, buying himself a few seconds to set his game face back in place. He should *not* be jealous that his dog had kissed Hazel before he had.

Hazel scratched Gunny near his tail before turning away to the counter to open a cookie jar filled with green chews. "Want a treat?" Gunny's tail thumped against Burke's leg in anticipation of his reward. "Who's the best patient ever? That's right, Gunny. It's you." Hazel held up her hand, giving the dog a command. "Sit. Good boy. Here you go." He liked that she respected the dog's training and didn't simply spoil him with treats and petting, although his

K-9 partner had no problem being a hand-fed couch potato when his vest was off and he was off duty. Hazel rubbed Gunny around the ears one last time before opening the door onto the hallway that led to the lobby. Burke was pleased, too, that the dog's ears were no longer sensitive to the touch and itching like crazy. Dr. Coop did good work. She smiled. "Come on, you two. I'll walk you out."

Gunny automatically heeled, noticing the people, pets and displays of food and treats and other supplies around them, without showing much interest or taking his focus off Burke as they followed Hazel to the front counter. The big dog paused once to touch noses and match tail wags with Cleo, the three-legged, one-eyed miniature schnauzer who trotted around the counter to greet him. Hazel brought the smaller senior dog to work with her every day, where she lounged in her own bed beside the reception staff or worked as something of a goodwill ambassador around the veterinary clinic. Cleo had earned the strands of white showing in her gray muzzle, and she made it her business to greet favorite customers and new patients. Gunny was definitely on Cleo's favorites list. If Burke was given to fanciful imaginings, he'd think Gunny and Cleo had a bit of a crush on each other, judging by the way they rubbed against each other and made quick work of the whole tail-sniffing scenario.

Hazel Cooper, however, *was* prone to fanciful imaginings with the animals she worked with. As Cleo danced between her legs and batted at Gunny, encouraging him to play, Hazel reached down to pet the schnauzer's flank. "That's right, your boyfriend's here."

"Cleo does know she's fixed, doesn't she?" Burke teased. "Her flirting's not going to do her any good. Nothing's going to happen between these two."

"A girl can still look, can't she?"

When Hazel straightened, her gaze traveled up his stomach, chest and jaw to meet his. A flare of heat passed between them, and Burke's mouth went dry. Well, hell. What kind of mixed signal was that? The good doctor had checked him out. So it was okay for her to look, too? But she still wanted him to keep things professional and friendly between them? Maybe the rules of dating had changed too much since he'd last taken the plunge and he had no business even considering acting upon the connection the two of them shared.

Whatever spark she'd felt, she either dutifully ignored it or else it fizzled out. Hazel leaned over the counter to speak to the receptionist at her computer. "Go ahead and send today's bill to the police department," she instructed, before tilting her gaze up to his again. Burke liked that about her, too—that she made direct eye contact with him and didn't mince words. At six feet two, he figured he was about eight inches taller than she was, but the veterinarian never let that deter her from meeting his gaze, no matter how close they stood. "I don't need to see Gunny again until his next checkup or shots are due. Just be sure to keep his ears clean. And if he starts shaking his head or scratching again, you can use more of that medicated ointment I gave you. Call me, of course, if that doesn't take care of it."

"Will do." He was out of excuses for hanging around the vet clinic and Dr. Coop. Gunny had a clean bill of health. He'd stretched out on the floor and Cleo had propped her two front paws on his back, as though standing tall on her big buddy's shoulders made her a big dog, too. But even though Gunny was enjoying the pseudo-massage of the other dog walking on him, Burke was on the clock. And he had nothing left to report on the background investigation he'd done on Hazel's ex-husband. He pulled his KCPD ball cap from his back pocket and adjusted it over his closely cropped hair. "Better get back to work. I'll keep you posted if I find out anything more about—" he glanced around at all the people in the front waiting area "—that matter we discussed."

"Thank you," she mouthed, no doubt appreciating his discretion about keeping her private affairs private. "See you next time." Burke nodded. She pursed her lips together and made a noisy kissing sound to get her dog's attention. "Cleo, come."

After a tumble onto her back leg, Cleo quickly righted herself and trotted over to her mistress to be petted. Then Hazel picked up the stack of mail the receptionist set on the counter for her and started sorting through the letters, a couple of magazines and a padded mailer. Burke had turned to the door and pulled Gunny into a heeling position when he heard the soft gasp behind him.

"Dr. Coop?" He turned to see the lighter envelopes floating to the floor alongside the small package Hazel had dropped. "Hazel?" Her panicked gaze darted up to his when he used her first name. What the hell? He glanced down at the mess around her feet, searching for one that looked like a threat. "Did you get another letter?"

With a curt nod to him and a forced smile for everyone else in the room, she shook off her momentary panic and squatted down to gather up the envelopes and magazines. "Maybe. I don't know. There's no return address on that package, and the label is typed. Like the others. But there haven't been any packages before." Like Cleo, Gunny was curious why his favorite doctor was down at his level. The dogs sniffed at Hazel, sniffed the scattered mail…and then Gunny sat. "The others have gone to my home address. This is the first one to come here." Burke's concern that some anonymous turd had upset Hazel again morphed into something far graver when Gunny tipped his long brown snout up to him. Ah, hell. "Maybe it's nothing. Not everybody puts a return address—"

"Don't touch another thing." He grasped Hazel by the arm and lifted her to her feet, placing her behind him as he backed away from the counter. He scooped Cleo up with one hand and put her in Hazel's arms when the smaller dog tried to sniff the package, too.

"What are you doing?"

Burke pulled out his badge and held it up to identify himself to the entire room in a clear, concise voice. "I need everyone's attention. I'm Sergeant

Jedediah Burke, KCPD." He swiveled his gaze to include everyone in the lobby. "I need everyone to stay exactly where you are. Does everybody have control of their animals? Don't. Move."

Hazel hugged Cleo to her chest. "Burke?"

"That includes you. Stay put. Don't let the dog down." He nudged her back another step before clipping his badge back onto his belt and leading Gunny out the double glass doors.

When he came back in with the dog, he was aware of fearful stares, questioning looks and a nervous laugh from behind the counter. But nobody spoke, nobody questioned his orders as he let Gunny nose his way around the shelves of dog food, a cat meowing in its carrier, then along the edge of the front counter and back to the pile of mail on the floor.

Gunny alerted again when he reached the padded envelope, sitting back on his haunches and tilting his nose up to Burke.

Burke swore. He slipped Gunny's chew toy reward between his teeth and pulled him away from the envelope, praising him for doing his job.

Gunny's nose was as reliable as clockwork.

Hazel's love letters had just taken a very sinister, very deadly turn.

He pulled his radio off his belt and summoned Dispatch before looking down into Hazel's worried expression. He couldn't spare more than a glance to reassure her he hadn't completely gone off his gourd because he needed to act.

"I need everybody—people, animals—to evacu-

ate the building ASAP." He swiveled his gaze to include every staff member and client in the lobby. "I
want you all at least twenty yards away, in the front
parking lot. Turn off your phones. Do not send a text.
Do not call anyone." He looked to Hazel again because he knew he could rely on her to keep her head
and get the job done, even if she was frightened. "I'll
need a head count to make sure everyone is where
they should be."

"Of course." She waved the three receptionists
out of their seats while Burke positioned himself to
blockade the padded envelope, so that no one would
accidentally step on it as they hurried to do their
boss's bidding. "Linda. Get on the headset, get the
staff out of the back rooms. Tell everyone I want
them in the parking lot. Get the animals we're boarding on leashes and put them in the kennel runs out
back. Todd." She pointed to the swinging door as the
young man came out of an examination room. "Get
the two dogs we neutered this morning out of Recovery. Ashley—"

"I'll take care of the customers out here, Mom."
Hazel's daughter didn't hesitate to do her mother's
bidding, but fear was clearly stamped on her face
when she stopped in front of Burke and asked,
"What's going on?"

"It's just a precaution," Burke answered, nodding
toward the exit and urging her to keep moving. "Call
it a fire drill."

"There's a fire?" she whispered. "The alarm didn't
go off."

Hazel pressed Cleo into Ashley's arms and turned her to the front door. "It's okay, sweetie. Just do as Burke says. I'll go through the exam rooms."

Ashley nodded, then held out her arm to escort one of their elderly clients to the parking lot, where customers, patients and staff were gathering. Hazel opened the doors to each examination room and led the pets and people into the lobby.

"Twenty yards out," Burke reminded Todd as the young man hurried by with the dogs from the recovery room.

Todd spared a worried glance for Hazel as she stepped back from the double doors at the front vestibule. "Dr. Coop, you coming?"

"I'll be right there." Hazel peered through the glass, counting her staff members and assuring their safety before she turned around and came back to find Burke relaying details to the dispatcher. Normally he would have used his cell phone, but he couldn't risk using a wireless signal until he knew more.

"What's going on?" she demanded the moment he signed off. She needed an explanation to fit his evacuation order and calm the panic caused by the sudden mass exodus. "I know there's no fire. I heard the dispatcher say she was sending a unit. Who's coming?"

"The bomb squad."

Her eyes widened before dropping her gaze to the unmarked package. "A bomb? I thought it was just another… I hadn't gotten a letter this week. I'd hoped Aaron would stop once his parole officer spoke with him. Did that just piss him off?" He could tell she was hoping he'd say this was a false alarm when she tilted her face back to his. "You think he sent a bomb to my clinic? With all these people? These innocent animals?"

Burke reached down to rub Gunny's head. "Gunny alerted there was an explosive. That nose of his is never wrong." Taking Hazel by the elbow, he escorted her to the vestibule. He wished he could tell her there was nothing to worry about, that it was okay to smile and erase the fear he read in her eyes. "I need you outside, too. Gunny and I have to clear the building."

"But…" She planted her feet and refused to leave. "That's what the bomb squad is for, right? Shouldn't you have backup?" She splayed her hand at the middle of his chest. His heart leaped against her urgent touch. "Or body armor?"

"Go. It's what we do." He cupped her cheek and jaw in his hand. "But I need you to be safe before I can go to work. I need you to be in charge out there."

She nodded. Then, with those green eyes tilted up to his, she covered his hand with hers. "I'll see you outside," she vowed, as if her will could guarantee that they'd be reunited.

Bombs didn't come with any kind of guarantee. He'd seen far too many of them when his Army unit had been deployed to the Middle East. He'd seen more than he'd ever imagined stateside now that he wore this uniform. The volatility of the explosives Gunny had been trained to detect meant, by their very nature, there were no guarantees he could give.

He traded a curt nod before opening the door and sending her out.

Burke watched her join Ashley and that ponytailed vet tech before he felt the eager tension radiating up Gunny's lead into his hand. The dog thought bomb detections and building searches were a sport that would end with a tug-of-war game with his favorite toy if he successfully found his target. But Burke knew just how serious this job could be.

Backup was en route. But KCFD and the bomb squad couldn't do a damn thing to help unless he could tell them that there were no other explosives, no other potential casualties on-site, no perp lying in wait to take out a first responder. Their job was to make sure it was safe to enter the building to deal with whatever was in the package that some pervert had sent Hazel.

"Gunny, *voran*!" Burke tugged on Gunny's leash and gave him the search command in German. "Come on, boy. Let's go to work."

Chapter Three

"Lookin' good, Shadow." Hazel checked the incision on the black Lab she'd neutered that morning, adjusted the E-collar around her neck and petted her chest before closing the door to her kennel.

The big dog yawned and laid her head down on the cushion inside the kennel, relaxing as though she'd come for a day at the spa instead of a desexing operation and a bomb threat. Hazel wished she could slough off the stress of the day so easily. With the fire department and police cars that had blocked traffic around the clinic gone, and no one left from the bomb squad here except for Burke's friend Justin Grant, she should be breathing a sigh of relief. All but one of her clients had rescheduled appointments and left once the police had deemed it safe to move their vehicles out of the parking lot. The animals she was responsible for were all safe. The members of her staff, although understandably shaken by the threat, had gone back to their duties, like the professionals they were, to finish out the workday as soon as the first responders had informed them it was safe to come back inside the building.

But *safe* was a relative term.

Hazel couldn't help thinking that the vial of C-4 pellets and a trigger mechanism wrapped in a bunch of colorful unconnected wires were meant to do more than scare her. Why would a man who'd write love letters—no matter how unnervingly obsessive they were—send her a package of bomb parts? Did he think being afraid would make her turn to him for comfort? Was he angry because she hadn't responded the way he wanted to his professions of love and desire? Not that she could respond one way or another to a man who refused to identify himself. And if the package had come from Aaron, was he still so angry with her that he'd send what could only be construed as a death threat?

Sixteen years ago he hadn't been so courteous to give her that kind of warning.

For a few nightmarish seconds, Hazel's breath locked up in her chest as she relived flashes of memory from that horrific night when Aaron had done what he thought was necessary to stop her from testifying against him.

Even though there were no words, there was a message for her in that package.

If only she knew what it meant, and who had sent it, she could devise coping and security strategies—she could turn his name over to KCPD and move on with the useful, contented life she'd created for herself and her daughters. She'd dealt with death threats against her and her daughters before, years ago when Aaron's crimes had been discovered, and the people who'd trusted him had lost everything. Hell, she'd dealt with Aaron, who'd been even more frightening. But how did she equate *I want you* with the promise of violence and death?

What had she ever done that was so horribly wrong that someone wanted to do this to her? Again.

Hazel pushed to her feet. She hugged her arms around her waist and leaned against the frame of the kennel wall, closing her eyes for a few moments to take in the familiar sounds and smells of her clinic. From Shadow's nasal breathing to the rustle and vocalizations of the other animals settling into their kennels for the evening, from the stringent tang of antiseptic cleanser used on her equipment to the more earthy scents of the animals themselves—this was her world, her safe zone, the place where she felt most at home. She was the authority here, in charge of her own schedule, her own destiny. She was surrounded by her daughter and friends and work she loved. Being here helped to center her and call up the strength that would get her through this nightmare of being the focus of someone's dangerously obsessive attention.

She inhaled deeply, intending to release a calming breath, when the air around her changed its scent. She opened her eyes a split second before Todd Mizner reached for her and pulled her lightly against his chest.

The younger man's supportive hug startled more

than it comforted. "You okay, Dr. Coop? That was a big scare, wasn't it?"

If she hadn't felt the trembling through his arms, she might have chastised him for the unwelcome contact. But Todd was probably as rattled by the idea of a bomb threat as she'd been. Like some men, maybe he wouldn't admit his fear, but he took comfort by helping someone else deal with hers. Instead of pushing him away, she settled her hands at his waist and let him hang on to her for a few seconds before stepping back. "I'm fine, Todd. Thanks for checking. Fortunately, no one was hurt. We've reopened for business. I think we'll be fine."

He adjusted his glasses on his nose before frowning at her response. "We've all got your back here. You know that, right?"

"I know that, Todd. Thank you." She squeezed his arm and patted it just like she had the dog and moved on to the next kennel to check her patient there. "Are the staff doing okay?" she asked. "How are you holding up?"

"I'm not the one that package was addressed to." He reached in beside her to adjust the dog's E-collar while she inspected the sutures, brushing his shoulder against hers. Although she often made accidental contact with the vet techs when they were working together with an animal, Todd's next words made her think she needed to have a conversation with him about the difference between *friendly* and *too friendly* when it came to his interactions with the female staff here at the clinic. "You know, if you want to go get a glass of wine or something to unwind and let the tension go after work, I'd be happy to take you someplace."

"Todd—"

When she started to refuse, he put his hands up in surrender, retreating a step to give her the space he must have just realized he'd invaded again. "A bunch of us could go. Celebrate life and all that after our close call this afternoon."

Hazel shut the kennel door before answering. "No, thank you. If you and some of the others want to celebrate, that's great. I love hearing that you all are supporting each other. But I think I'll be heading straight home once this day is over. I'm exhausted."

"You sure?" His disappointment in her refusal to join him, or them, was evident for a few seconds before he rallied with a smile. "Maybe another time."

She made a point of checking her watch instead of replying to the open-ended invitation. "You'd better get those dogs we're boarding out for their last run before we close up shop."

"Anything you say, boss lady."

After Todd left to do her bidding, Hazel went through her office and the workrooms in the back to grab her purse, turn off lights and close the doors that connected to each exam room. Maybe there hadn't been anything all that unusual about Todd's concern for her. By the time she reached the reception area, her staff had all the computers shut down, and the appointment schedule and prescription orders ready for the next morning. One by one they gave her a hug and wished her good-night, repeating Todd's invitation to join them for a celebration-slash-commiseration drink. Hazel thanked them all, commended them for keeping their heads in a crisis and ordered them to have some fun.

The sky was gray with twilight and the air smelled of ozone ahead of the promised storm by the time she hooked Cleo to her leash, locked the front doors and headed down the ramp to her truck. Two other trucks remained in the parking lot, both with the distinctive black-and-white markings that identified them as KCPD vehicles. Her gaze instantly went to the broad-shouldered man leaning back against the K-9 truck with his arms crossed over his wide chest in an easy, deceptively relaxed stance. Burke was in the middle of a conversation with the senior officer from the bomb squad she'd met earlier, Justin Grant. Clearly, the two men were friends, judging by the laughter they shared. Justin was younger— blond, slightly taller than Burke, and built like a lanky distance runner. Of course, most men seemed slighter standing next to Burke's muscular build.

Hazel's eyes widened as the surprising observation popped into her head, and she hurried Cleo over to a grassy patch in the landscaping around the parking lot for the dog to take care of business before the drive home. What was she doing? Comparing other men against Burke's standard? Officer Grant was a handsome man, but she had barely noticed him once she'd caught sight of Burke. She wasn't naive enough to deny that she was attracted to Burke on some subconscious level—any healthy woman would be. But when had her conscious thoughts become so attuned to the rugged police sergeant?

Once Burke caught sight of her and Cleo, he straightened away from the truck and smiled. Maybe that was what the distraction was—Burke's attention always seemed to shift to her whenever they were in the same space together. That could explain her hyperawareness of him. Why wouldn't she be equally aware of a man whose focus was concentrated on her?

That was all this was—alert cop, polite man, a few errant hormones appreciating the attention after so many years on her own—and the last years before that with Aaron, when she'd been reduced to invisibility one day, verbal whipping dog the next and, ultimately, the target of his desperation. She and Burke had shared a special friendship from the time when she'd first started working with him and the other K-9 officers at KCPD. He respected her. He was a calm presence. Sometimes he even made her laugh. Her self-preserving guard was a little off after those love letters and the events of today, making her thoughts a little scattered, her instincts a little sharper. There was no need to worry that she might be developing different, deeper feelings for him. Tomorrow she'd wake up with her strength and survival instincts intact, and she could push those feelings into the background, where she needed them to stay.

"Cleo, come." With the dog down to fumes now after staking out several spots, Hazel calmed her off-kilter thoughts and walked past her truck to join the

two men. Cleo darted ahead of her, eager to investigate them, or perhaps catching Gunny's scent as
the big dog lounged in his air-conditioned kennel in
the back seat of Burke's truck. Cleo sniffed Officer
Grant's shoes before propping her two front paws
against Burke's knee, wobbling on her back leg and
wagging her stump of a tail. "Easy, girl," she said.

"Dr. Coop." Justin Grant chuckled as he nodded
a greeting, amused by the dog's favoritism. "Who's
this little diva?"

"Cleo. She was hit by a car and left by the side
of the road. She was with us in recovery for a long
time, and since no one claimed her, my staff adopted
her and made her the clinic mascot. I get the honor
of chauffeuring her home for the evenings. And she
has a crazy crush on this big galoot."

"You got everything locked up?" Burke asked.
He knelt to scratch Cleo around the ears, easing the
schnauzer's manic energy with his deep voice and
large hands. "She probably smells Gunny on me.
Makes me a hit with all the furry ladies." He talked
to the dog, working his trainer magic. "Chill, little
one. Gunny worked hard all afternoon and needs his
rest. Maybe you can play with him tomorrow. That's
a good girl."

By the time he was done talking, the three-legged
dog had rolled onto her side and was panting while
Burke rubbed her tummy. Some of the tension inside
Hazel eased, too, hearing that soothing, low-pitched
voice. She'd probably be panting, too, if he whispered
little praises to her and stroked her skin like that.

Hazel quickly turned away as a different sort of tension seized her. Where were these sexual thoughts coming from? Why was she allowing herself to react to Burke in a way she never had before? Once Ashley had put those thoughts about flirting and feelings into her head, she hadn't been able to compartmentalize her emotions the way she usually did. She really needed to find out who was behind these threats and get the normalcy of her familiar, predictable life back.

Studiously ignoring the man kneeling beside her and indulging her spoiled dog, Hazel tilted her chin to Justin. "You're certain it's safe to resume business as usual tomorrow morning?"

"Yes, ma'am." The younger officer seemed unaware of the embarrassment heating her cheeks, or else he was too polite to mention it. "Our search teams found nothing you need to worry about except for that envelope."

"An envelope filled with bomb-making parts," she clarified, still in a bit of shock that something so dangerous had traveled through the mail and ended up in her place of work, where she, her daughter and so many of her friends were.

"In this case, parts are just parts," Justin assured her. "Nothing was rigged to detonate. C-4 requires an electric charge through a triggering device like a blasting cap or detonator cord. The small explosion triggers the larger one. As unsettling as receiving a gift like that might be, nothing was going to happen. Even if you struck a match to it, it would burn, not explode. All the same, we've got the C-4 secured, and the envelope is on its way to the evidence locker."

"Nobody sends explosives through the mail for no reason." Burke pushed to his feet beside her, his shoulders filling up her peripheral vision, making a mockery of her efforts to ignore her awareness of him. "This perp has broken the law just by putting that package in a mail slot and lying about its contents. That's a big risk to take."

Justin nodded his agreement. "The sender may be an expert in explosives who knew the device wouldn't work, and this was either a gag or a warning of some kind. Probably the latter, given those letters you mentioned."

Hazel shivered, feeling the electricity in the air dotting her skin with goose bumps. She was swallowed up by the cold front being pushed ahead of the pending storm, and she hugged her arms around her waist, wishing she had more than her scrubs on to keep her warm. "Someone thinks this is funny?"

She shouldn't have been surprised to feel Burke's arm slide around her shoulders or his hand rubbing up and down her arm. "From the perp's perspective, not yours. Maybe he wants you to know how serious his feelings are for you. Or he's hoping you'll be scared enough to turn to him for comfort."

She was equally surprised at how easy it was to lean against Burke's warmth and strength as the unsettling chill consumed her. "The man doesn't even have the guts to tell me who he is. Does he really believe that threatening me is going to make me ignore the ick factor of those letters and fall in love with him?"

"Another possibility is that he's a novice who has no clue what he's messing with and didn't realize that the contents couldn't go off." Justin shook his head, as though he liked that possibility even less. "I hate to think that he'll keep trying until he gets it right."

"Don't worry, Doc." Burke squeezed her shoulders a little tighter. "Gunny and I are at your service whenever you need us."

She squeezed his hand where it rested on her shoulder. "Cleo and I appreciate it. Thanks." At the mention of her name, the little dog got to her feet and danced around her legs. She wished she could share the old girl's enthusiasm for this conversation. "So you think he'll try again?" Hazel asked the younger man.

"If he's already escalated from letter writing to threats like that, then yeah, as long as he has access to the right equipment, I doubt this is a onetime thing."

Hazel lifted her chin at the grim pronouncement. Sixteen years ago, at the height of her ex-husband's trial, she'd been bombarded with hate mail, anonymous phone calls and threats against her and her daughters—as if she was guilty by association for the way Aaron had destroyed so many lives. If only they'd known how thoroughly he'd destroyed hers, they might have felt sympathy rather than hate. But other than being jostled and spit on by a courthouse crowd, and her daughters being bullied at school— the last straw that had sealed her decision to testify against Aaron and finalize their divorce—none of those threats had ended in violence like this. Not the kind where people died. "He's trying to get my attention. He's probably too much of a coward to actually hurt me."

The two men exchanged a look as though her optimistic assertion was naive. But she wasn't about to explain to a man she'd just met why she had so little naivete left about the world—just a foolish hope that she'd already lived through the worst the world had to offer, and a belief that the future had to be better.

"I hope that's the case," Justin said. "In the meantime, I'll keep working the investigation from my end. See if I can find out where that C-4 came from. The guy has to have connections to construction jobs or the military—or the black market—in order to get his hands on that grade of explosive." He reached out to shake hands with Burke. "I'll keep you posted on what I find out."

Burke nodded his thanks. "Say hi to Emilia and the kids. When is number three due?"

"This summer."

"You know scientists found out what causes that, don't you?"

Justin grinned at the teasing. "Don't lecture me about making babies, old man. You know you love being JJ's godfather."

"I do. Tell him I'll bring Gunny by again sometime for the two of them to play."

"Will do." Justin looked to Hazel and extended his hand. "Dr. Coop. I'm sorry this happened."

"Thank you, Officer Grant."

"Justin." As they shook hands, he nodded toward Burke. "If you're hanging out with this guy, I imagine we'll be crossing paths again."

Although she didn't think that dealing with bomb threats and disturbing letters or even canine ear infections qualified as "hanging out," Hazel realized she had spent more time with Burke in the past week than she had over the past two months. Did Justin think there was something more going on between her and Burke, too? First, Ashley had claimed Burke was flirting with her. And now Justin had practically labeled them a couple. She'd better be careful. Leaning on Jedediah Burke could become a habit she wouldn't want to break. Did she imagine his hand tightening around her shoulder briefly before she decided it might be wiser to break contact and step away from him?

And why was that subtle pressure all it took to keep her snugged to his side?

Justin backed toward his truck. "You need anything else from me, give me a call."

"Roger that." Burke's arm was still around her shoulders as Justin drove out of the parking lot.

The breeze was picking up as Cleo tugged on the leash, apparently ready to do some more exploring if Hazel didn't offer her a comfortable place to nap and Burke wasn't going to be petting her anymore. The wind held an unexpected bite as she moved away from Burke's warmth to let the dog reach the grass.

Was the chill she felt physical or mental or both? She rubbed her free hand up and down her arm and turned her face to the sky to see the layers of clouds darting by. The wind whipped her bangs across her eyes and lifted the short waves on top of her head. "Looks like we're going to get a storm."

Burke's sigh was a deep rumble through the air behind her. "Are we reduced to that now? Talking about the weather like a couple of acquaintances who barely know each other?" He stepped up beside her, his callused fingers a soothing caress as he brushed the hair out of her eyes. He repeated the same gentle stroke across her forehead and along her temple before cupping the side of her jaw and letting his fingers curve around the back of her neck. "Promise me one thing. You'll never be afraid to speak what's on your mind to me."

She nodded. "Same here. You've always been a straight shooter with me, and I don't want that to change."

His fingertips pulled against the tension at the nape of her neck. "Then, in the spirit of honesty…you look worn-out. You doin' okay?"

"Nothing that a good night's sleep and feeling safe again won't cure."

"Anything I can do to help?"

Hazel had closed her eyes against the heavenly massage, until she realized she was just as shamelessly addicted to his touch as Cleo had been. She blinked her eyes open to find Burke studying her expression, waiting for her answer. "I thought I'd have some answers by now—that this obsession would end, not escalate." She reached up to wrap her fingers around his wrist, stilling his kneading long enough to share an embarrassing truth. "What if I can't handle this? I'm not as young as I was when I had to deal with this kind of emotional chaos before. And it nearly broke me back then."

"You're not alone this time." He tugged against her neck, pulling her into his chest and winding his arms around her. "I assume you're referring to that mess with your ex?"

She nodded.

He might not know the details, but he knew enough to understand that she'd been put through hell and had survived. "Maybe you've traded some of those youthful energy reserves for life experience. You'll be smarter about dealing with this mess than you were the last one. And if you are intimating in any way, shape or form that you are over the hill, and not strong or vibrant or able to deal with what life's throwing at you right now, I'm going to have to pick a fight with you."

She huffed a laugh at the compliment. "Have I ever told you how good you are for my ego, Sergeant Burke?"

"Just being a straight shooter, ma'am."

The inner voice that reminded her to maintain a professional distance from the veteran cop grew weaker with every breath she took. She settled against him, soothed by the strong beat of his heart beneath her ear. Her arms snuck around his waist as he nestled his chin against the crown of her hair and surrounded her in his abundant heat. She flattened her hands against his strong back and admitted to the tingling she felt in the tips of her breasts as they responded to the friction of her body pressed against his. God, he felt good. Solid, masculine. He smelled even better. If she wasn't gun-shy about starting a relationship with him, she could see herself falling for Burke far too easily. If he could work such magic with his hands, she could only imagine how sexy and addictive his kisses would be. Would he be gentle? Authoritative? Some heady mix in between?

As for sex... Her experience with Aaron had been all about the bells and whistles after the initial bloom of young love had faded. Just like her trust, their physical relationship had deteriorated to mechanics and trying too hard and finally to disappointment and neglect. Other than her husband, she hadn't had any partners. She had a feeling that, like the man himself, getting physical with Burke would be straightforward. *I want you. I'll make it good. Let's do this.*

Her breasts weren't the only part of her stinging with wakening desire now. Fantasizing about Jedediah Burke, imagining something more between them, reminded Hazel that she was a sexual being who'd denied her needs for far too long. Her marriage had crumbled, and she'd gone into survivor mode. She'd concentrated on being a mother and father to her girls, as well as a successful business owner who could support them and their dreams. She'd found solace in her work and a purposeful way to atone for the damage Aaron had done to the world by helping the animals in her care. But somewhere along the way she'd forgotten what it felt like to be held by a man, to be desired by one, to want something that was just for her.

She parted her lips as the heat building inside her demanded an outlet. As restlessness replaced her fatigue, she shifted her cheek against Burke's shoulder. Even his beard stubble catching a few strands of her hair and tugging gently against her scalp felt like a caress, but she couldn't seem to make herself pull away from his embrace. She opened her eyes to focus on the KCPD logo on the side of his truck, reminding herself why she'd turned to Burke in the first place. "Haven't you already done enough today? If you hadn't been here, I might have opened that package."

But then he pressed a kiss to her temple. His arms tightened imperceptibly around her. "Just doin' my job, Doc."

Hazel shivered at the deep, husky tone, but not because she was chilled by the cooling weather. Her body was responding to the call of his. Were Ashley's observations right? Could this strong, kind man want something more between them, too?

"Haze…"

She leaned back against his arms and tipped her face up to his descending mouth. "Burke, I..."

A beep from her purse interrupted whatever mistake she'd been about to make. A text. She was equal parts relieved and disappointed as she pressed her palms against his shoulders and backed out of his arms. She needed a good friend more than she needed another failed relationship right now. And she didn't imagine the kiss that had almost happened would have resulted in anything else but a complication neither of them needed.

"Sorry." She reached into her purse to pull out her cell phone. "Just in case it's a patient emergency."

Burke turned away, scrubbing his palm over his jaw as she unlocked the screen. She wasn't sure if that was frustration or relief that left him rolling the tension from his neck and shoulders. Instead of worrying about his reaction to that almost kiss when she wasn't sure of what she herself was feeling, she pulled up the text.

She didn't recognize the number or name of any patient, but, needing the distraction, she opened it, anyway. It was an animated meme with a caption. She recognized the familiar shape of her younger daughter's red car and smiled for a moment, thinking Polly had sent her a funny message to cheer her up.

But the number wasn't Polly's. Hazel frowned in confusion. Confusion quickly gave way to a fear that hollowed out her stomach.

The words that accompanied the picture were neither her daughter's nor funny.

I'm coming for you and everything you care about.

Don't make the mistake of thinking I'm not a threat, or that I'm not watching your every waking moment.

You're mine.

The picture exploded with cartoonish fireworks that faded away to reveal the burned-out frame of an automobile.

"Burke..." A mama bear's anger blazed behind her eyes, making her dizzy for a moment. She swung around and held up the awful image. "Burke!"

She showed him the text and he cursed.

He double-checked the time stamp and cursed again, swiveling his gaze 360 degrees around the empty parking lot and light traffic on the street beyond. The strip mall across the street had cars near a restaurant and waiting in line at the drive-through bank. The graying sky reflected in all the windows, keeping her from seeing if anyone was spying on her from inside one of the shops. "He just now sent this. He's got eyes on you. Or he knows your schedule, knows your routine."

Hazel looked, too, but she didn't see anyone staring at her, no one sitting in his car and pointing at her, laughing at how easily he could get under her skin and upset her. "Polly owns a Kia just like that.

I'm sure she drove it to work this morning. She's at Saint Luke's Hospital, working and taking classes." Hazel watched the message play again, willing for some sort of clue to appear and reveal her tormentor's identity. "Is he threatening my baby…?"

Whether she was ten years old or twenty-one, her younger daughter would always be her baby. And a sick message like this text did more to frighten Hazel than any anonymous love letter or vial of C-4 could.

Burke clamped his hand around her upper arm and pulled her to the passenger door of his truck. "Get in. Call Polly. We're going to the hospital."

"I can drive."

"No." He opened the door.

"No? She's my daughter. I have to—"

His big hands spanned her waist and he picked her up and set her inside. He bent down to pick up Cleo and plopped the dog onto her lap before she could climb back out. Then he blocked the open door, meeting her eye to eye. "You're angry right now. And you're scared for your child. I don't want you driving while you're on your phone and worried about her."

She had to look away from the intensity in those dark brown eyes. She didn't need to argue for her independence. He was making sense. She thanked him with a nod. "Good point."

He jogged around to get in behind the wheel and started the truck. "Give me the number again."

Hazel rattled off the caller's ID while Burke backed out of the parking space and picked up his radio to call Dispatch. Gunny sat up the moment his handler had climbed into the truck and whined quietly in the back as they pulled into traffic and picked up speed. Cleo was on her feet, wanting to touch noses with the working dog through the grate separating them, but Hazel wrapped her arms around the schnauzer to keep her in her lap.

Burke identified himself and reported the text as a bomb threat before warning Dispatch to alert the bomb squad and KCFD. Then he recited the phone number and asked her to run a trace on it. After he signed off, he glanced at Hazel. "They'll put an investigator on tracking down that cell number, although I'm guessing it'll be a burner phone." He reached out to rub his hand over the top of Cleo's head. "Once we know Polly's okay—and she will be okay—you and I are going downtown and filing a full report on this harassment campaign."

"Thank you."

He slid his hand along Cleo's back until he caught Hazel's hand and squeezed it. "You and your girls will be safe, Doc. I promise." Returning both hands to the wheel, he nodded toward her phone. "Call."

Hazel punched in her younger daughter's number while the truck sped along Front Street toward downtown. A mist was spitting on the windshield now, and Burke turned on the wipers, along with his flashing lights and siren as they ran into rush hour traffic.

"Hey, Mom. What's up?"

It was a relief to hear Polly's voice. "Are you at the hospital?"

"Where else would I be?" Polly asked. Hazel heard

voices and laughter in the background, as though her daughter was safely surrounded by friends. "It's my long day. Classes. Work. My evening volunteer seminar starts in half an hour."

The clouds blinked with lightning, and thunder rumbled overhead, the coming storm adding to the urgency of the moment. "Don't leave the building," Hazel warned. "We're on our way to you."

"We?"

"Sergeant Burke is driving me."

"Ooh, yum." She heard Polly excuse herself from whomever she was with, and the background noise quieted. "Sergeant Hottie McHotterson, who loves dogs as much as you do? Whose broad shoulders fill out his uniform like a man half his age? That Sergeant Burke?"

Hazel groaned, glad she didn't have the call on speakerphone, but she couldn't keep her gaze from sliding across the cab of the truck to verify her daughter's observation. She tried to make her next breath a sigh of relief. If Polly could tease her about her dating life, or lack thereof, then she had to be fine. "You've been talking to your sister."

"There might have been some cahootenizing over a couple of glasses of wine last weekend. You do know we both like him, right, Mom? If you ever decide you want to date again, Sergeant Burke would be on our approved list."

She wasn't having this discussion again. She needed to focus on the problem at hand. "Did you drive your car to the hospital this morning?"

"Of course I did."

"Have you been outside since then?"

"No. I had classes. Went on rounds with Professor Owenson in the maternity ward. I saw the rain in the forecast, and it was clouding up, so I just grabbed a bite of dinner in the cafeteria instead of going back to the apartment." Good. Her daughters shared an apartment, and knowing Ashley had headed home after work, she was relieved to hear that her older daughter wouldn't accidentally run into the danger indicated by that text when she pulled into the parking lot behind their complex.

"Where is your car now?"

"In the west lot." Polly hesitated, no doubt picking up on the urgency in her voice. "Mom, is something wrong?"

"Stay inside the hospital. Do not go to your car for any reason."

Burke motioned for her to hold the phone up and put it on speaker. "Polly? Jedediah Burke here."

"Hey, Sarge. What's going on?"

"Do what your mom says, and contact hospital security to cordon off your car. Tell them not to touch anything. We'll be there in ten minutes." The rain was coming down in sheets now. Could he guarantee that? "First responders are on their way."

"Okay, now you're both scaring me," said Polly. Hazel recognized the tightness in her daughter's tone. "Does this have anything to do with the package Mom got in the mail today? Ashley texted me about it this afternoon."

"Possibly. I don't want to scare you, but I believe someone may have tampered with your car. At least with one that looks like yours."

"Tampered? What do you mean? Like someone let the air out of my tires?" Even over the noise of the storm and traffic, Hazel could hear her daughter's quickened breaths. "I'm heading down the Wornall Road hallway to the south windows. I parked aboveground today. I can see my car from... There it is. Right where I left it. I was here early enough to get a surface-level spot."

"Don't go to it," Hazel warned. "Stay inside until we get there."

"It's okay, Mom. I'm just look—" When Polly gasped and went silent, Hazel nearly screamed into the phone.

But like all the women in the Cooper family, she was a medical professional and knew that panicking wasn't going to help anyone. "Polly?"

"Sergeant? Mom? There's a guy in a black hoodie out there. He's walking around my car, looking in the windows." Polly's soft voice told Hazel her daughter was afraid. "I can't see his face. What's he doing out there with all this rain? Nobody else is—"

"Call security," Burke ordered. He raced through an intersection. Gunny whined with more excitement and Cleo barked.

"He's jogging away. He ran down the ramp into the parking garage. I can't see exactly where he went. I hear sirens—they're not ambulances. Maybe he heard them, too."

"Do what Burke says, sweetie. Contact security and stay inside. We'll be right there."

Hazel heard a muffled thump like thunder in the distance. Had the storm reached Saint Luke's, too?

"Oh, my God." She barely heard her daughter's whisper.

"Polly? Please tell me that was thunder."

Burke shook his head.

Hazel knew by the pace of her breathing that her daughter was running. "I'm on my way to the security desk now."

"You need to talk to me right now, young lady."

"I'm okay, Mom. But get here fast. My car just blew up."

Chapter Four

The rain was pouring by the time the Kansas City Fire Department had extinguished the flames of Polly's car, driving everyone but the crime scene technicians back inside the hospital. Cradling Cleo in her lap, Hazel sat in a chair in the carpeted lobby, absently petting Gunny, who dozed at her feet, eavesdropping on Burke, Justin Grant and a stone-faced firefighter named Matt Taylor, whom Hazel had learned was a younger brother to Pike Taylor, the K-9 officer who worked with Burke.

Once the police had finished interviewing her, Polly had insisted on checking in for the last half hour of her volunteer seminar. Hazel understood her need to stay focused on something other than the danger that had come far too close this evening. Plus, Polly had inherited Hazel's own workaholic tendencies and wanted to finish the job she'd promised to do. Her big sister, Ashley, had shown up minutes after Hazel and Burke had arrived, as worried about Polly as Hazel was. The two young women were so close. Polly had probably texted Ashley for moral support the moment she'd gotten off the phone with Hazel.

Although the stress of the day was wearing on her, Hazel felt better knowing her daughters were under the same roof as she was, and she could keep an eye on them both and know they were safe.

She'd relive those last few months with Aaron a hundred times before she'd let anyone hurt one of her daughters.

Cleo stirred in Hazel's lap, alert to every employee, patient or visitor who walked past. Unfazed by her own physical handicaps, it was almost as though the small dog was keeping watch over her mistress. Or maybe the one-eyed schnauzer was keeping watch over her big bruiser buddy, who panted quietly at Hazel's feet. Unless they were registered therapy animals, dogs, as a rule, weren't allowed inside the hospital. But no one seemed to mind the smell of wet dog on the premises tonight. Burke's Czech shepherd had done his job, alerting to the remnants of explosives inside the front wheel well of Polly's car, his sensitive nose picking up the scent even after the firefighters had soaked the vehicle with foam and the storm had set in while the first responders cleared the scene. With the help of three other bomb-sniffing dogs and their partners, Gunny and Burke had cleared every vehicle in the parking garage and the interior of Saint Luke's itself.

Polly's car had been specifically targeted. Matt Taylor said the fire had been contained to Polly's car, the fuel in her gas tank had accounted for most of the flames, and only minor damage had been inflicted on the nearby vehicles. And though the police and search dogs had determined there were no other explosives on the site to worry about, Hazel still worried.

Her *daughter* had been targeted.

Even now, hours after the initial explosion, knowing Polly hadn't been anywhere close to the bomb when it detonated, Hazel felt light-headed with an overwhelming dose of anger and fear.

If Polly hadn't had such a full day and hadn't decided to eat dinner at the hospital, she might have been in that car, stuck in rush hour traffic, when it exploded. Hazel's baby girl might be horribly injured or… Hazel fisted her fingers in Gunny's long, damp coat. She refused to even think the word.

Threatening *her* was one thing.

Going after her children was something else entirely.

The letters had been upsetting, yes—the bomb parts delivered to the clinic were unsettling. But even with seeking out Burke's help, she hadn't taken the whole stalking situation as seriously as she should have until today. Now her friends and employees and daughters had been drawn into this senseless terror campaign. Her protective mama-bear hackles were on high alert. She could no longer separate the threats from the rest of her life, praying they'd go away, hoping she could handle the situation herself. Now she intended to meet the enemy head-on—protect her daughters, protect her staff—identify the culprit and then sic Gunny and Burke and the rest of the KCPD on him.

Matt Taylor had shed his big reflective coat and helmet, and he stood with his hands propped at the waist of his insulated turnout pants. "If the explosive had been placed in the back near the gas tank, we'd be talking a different story. As it is, other than the shrapnel that dinged the neighboring cars, most of the damage came from the fuel burning. The gas tank never exploded."

Justin looked from Matt to Burke. "So again, either this guy doesn't know what he's doing with these explosives, or he's deliberately drawing this out—upping the stakes with each threat instead of going for maximum damage." His green-eyed gaze darted over to Hazel, indicating he knew she was listening in. Yes, the damage had been more than enough, considering they were talking about Polly's car. But she hoped that locking gazes with him indicated she wanted to hear the questions and answers they were discussing, even if the topic might upset her. "How did our perp know which vehicle to target? The DMV's not a public-access database."

"Because he's watching Hazel and her girls." Burke's chest expanded with an angry breath. "He's inserted himself into their lives somehow, even in a periphery way, so he can learn all he can about them—where they work, where they live, their routines, what they drive." He scrubbed his palm over the stubble shading his jaw. "I need to ferret this guy out. Find out why he's doing this to Hazel and put a stop to it."

"Look, what you and the dogs you train do is invaluable. But you're not a detective, old man," Justin cautioned him.

Burke's glare was part reprimand and all irritation at the reminder. But whether it was the job description or the nickname that he didn't find amusing, she couldn't tell. "If Gunny can find a bomb in a campus this size, then I can damn well find the perp who put it there." He shrugged some of the tension off his shoulders and made a concession. "I won't go cowboy on anybody. I'll keep Detectives Bellamy and Cartwright in the loop. As long as they do the same for me."

Cooper Bellamy and Seth Cartwright were the two detectives who'd come to Saint Luke's to take statements from her, Burke and Polly. Now that the CSIs had set up a protective tarp and fog lights around the shell of Polly's car, Bellamy and Cartwright were out in the rain, getting preliminary statements from the criminologists on the scene and meeting with the guards at the security gate in front of the hospital to see if any of them had glimpsed the man in the black hoodie and could provide a more detailed description of the guy or his vehicle.

Right now, with no traceable phone number, no return address on the letters, and no answers yet on where he'd obtained the bomb parts and explosives, Polly's description of an oversized man in a black hoodie and dark pants who disappeared inside the parking garage was the best they had to go on.

"Keep KCFD in the loop, too," Matt said, extending his hand to shake both Burke's and Justin's. "I'll get you the results from our arson investigator as soon as we know anything more concrete."

"Thanks, Matt."

Matt nodded to Hazel as he strode past. "Ma'am."

"Thank you, Mr. Taylor."

She followed him to the front doors with her gaze and saw the young firefighter exchange a look with her older daughter, Ashley. Although she didn't think they knew each other, Ashley gave him a friendly wave before he walked out into the rain and she returned to the animated conversation she was having on her cell phone.

Hazel's eyes narrowed at the observation. Could something as simple as a friendly wave she didn't remember be the cause of all this terror and destruction? Did some creep fancy himself in love with her because she'd smiled at him or been polite?

Hazel had made a point of not dating for years now. Aaron had given her plenty of reason to be wary of men she didn't know. But even if she had considered getting to know a new man in an intimate way, she hadn't. First, because her daughters had needed her and the stability of being home every night during and after Aaron's trial and the dissolution of their disastrous marriage. And more recently because those years of emotional self-preservation had become an ingrained habit. If she wasn't any better a judge of whom to trust and give her heart to than when she fell for Aaron Cooper, then what business did she have risking another relationship?

It was Survival 101. She didn't lead on any man who might be interested in her. She stated her rules, tried to let him down easy if he pushed for her to bend those rules and kept her heart at a safe distance.

Had she slipped somewhere? She had several platonic relationships with men—like Burke, clients, coworkers, friends. Had she missed a sign that one of them had deeper feelings for her? Had she subconsciously encouraged someone into thinking she cared for him with a wave or a smile or a thank-you?

He's inserted himself into their lives...

Burke's assertion clanged like a warning bell inside her head.

Who was Ashley talking to? Judging by her big smile and lively responses, it had to be a boyfriend—or someone she wanted to be her boyfriend. Did Hazel know whom her daughter was interested in now? She'd broken up with her last boyfriend because he'd gotten too serious too fast for her. And bless Ashley's outgoing, adventurous heart, she didn't have settling down to babies and white picket fences on her mind anytime soon. Ashley claimed they'd parted on good terms. But could a man who'd been talking marriage really be content to walk away after a breakup?

Hazel turned in her seat, looking in the opposite direction down the hallway leading to the employees' locker room. Polly's ponytail was curlier than Ashley's and a couple of shades darker, but just as easy to spot. She strolled down the hallway, sharing a conversation with an older man wearing tattered jeans and an ill-fitting Army jacket. They stopped before reaching the side exit to the employee parking lot and faced each other. His shaggy beard and faded ball cap on top of his longish gray hair led her to think he was one of the homeless patients her daughter worked with in her volunteer seminar. Polly had a big heart and a bone-deep drive to help anyone in need. Hazel had always been proud of Polly's calling to be of service to others.

But she startled Cleo with a silent jerk of protest when the man leaned over and hugged Polly. Hazel absentmindedly stroked the dog's head to apologize but wasn't feeling any calmer herself. She didn't know that man holding on to her younger daughter as though she was a lifeline. Not that she knew every patient, classmate or teacher of Polly's. But would a man like that fancy himself in love simply because Polly had tended his wound or offered him a smile?

Did Hazel have any men like that or Ashley's phone friend in her life?

Was that how a stalker was born?

Identifying the man behind the letters and explosives meant starting with a single question. Hazel intended to spend some time on the computer tonight, reading through her patient files to refresh her memory about her clients and the salespeople and consultants she did business with. She'd urge Polly and Ashley to do the same with their circles of friends, coworkers and acquaintances. But for now, she was going to find out who that man was with Polly. Plus, it would give her an opportunity to check in with her daughter to see how she was holding up after seeing her most expensive possession and means of transportation be destroyed.

A warm hand folded over Hazel's shoulder, and she yelped louder than Cleo had.

"Easy." Burke quickly drew his hand away and retreated a step. "Didn't mean to startle you. You okay?"

"Sorry." She pulled her focus from her speculative thoughts long enough to reorient herself in the moment. She grounded herself in Burke's narrowed brown eyes and leaned to one side to see the rest of the lobby behind him. "Justin left?"

"Yeah. Detective Bellamy said they recovered more of the bomb parts and wanted him to examine them before they bagged everything up for the lab." She nodded, glad to have all these professionals working to help her now but wishing they had more answers for her. "Bellamy said they've put out a BOLO on the guy Polly described."

"An oversized man in a black hoodie and dark pants is pretty generic, isn't it?"

"It is. But it's a place to start." He must have read the doubt in her expression. And he couldn't miss her gaze darting between her daughters and following the homeless man as he left Polly and strolled around the lobby to the front doors. "Are the girls okay? That guy bothering them?"

"Young women. Not girls anymore." Had the homeless man's gaze brushed across Ashley's back as he walked out into the rain? "And no. Not that I could see. He was talking to Polly. Probably a patient. I guess I'm suspicious of everyone now."

"Everyone?" Burke prompted, perhaps wondering if he and the other cops and firefighters he'd been talking to were on that suspect list.

"I just wish I knew who was responsible…" Hazel pushed to her feet, setting Cleo down on the carpet beside Gunny. She placed both leashes into Burke's hand. "Do you mind? I need to check on Polly. I can find out who that man is and get at least one question answered tonight."

"I'll keep an eye on Cleo." Burke tilted his head toward the effervescent blonde laughing into her phone. "I'll keep an eye her, too."

Burke's matter-of-fact promise kindled a warm ball of light inside her, chasing away the almost desperate feeling of helplessness that had left her on edge from the moment she'd dropped that package at the clinic. Did he have any idea how grateful she was for his steady presence and ability to take charge of a situation and get whatever action was needed done? He'd been strong when her own strength had faltered. Hazel knew she was lucky that he was a part of her life. She reached up and splayed her fingers against his chest, fingering the KCPD logo emblazoned there. Did she imagine the tremor that rippled across the skin and muscle beneath her hand? "I'm not sure how I would have gotten through today without you. Thank you."

He placed his hand over hers, holding it against the strong beat of his heart. "Just doin' my job."

She shook her head. "You've gone above and beyond the call of duty, Jedediah. How long have you been off the clock? And you're still here with me."

His dark brows arched above his eyes when she used his given name, and she realized she'd never called him that before. He'd always been the big boss of the K-9 unit, Burke. Or Sarge. Or Sergeant Burke.

She liked the rhythmic sound of his name on her tongue. "Is it okay if I call you that? Jedediah?"

"Yeah." His answer was a deep-pitched rumble that danced across all kinds of nerve endings and scattered her vows of friendship and keeping him arm's length from her heart. "Jedediah's good. Do I still have to call you Dr. Coop?"

Good gravy. This man could read the phone book or a grocery list in that voice, and her pulse would race a little faster.

"Of course not. Hazel's such an old-fashioned name, though—I almost always had a nickname. I was named after one of my grandmothers. I was always the only Hazel in class, surrounded by Lisas and Karens and Marys." She wiggled her fingers beneath his hand, tracing the *C* on his chest, idly speculating how a man in his fifties kept himself in such good shape. "I bet there weren't a lot of Jedediahs, either."

"You were unique. You still are."

Why did that sound more like a compliment than a commentary? Was he talking about more than her name? Was she?

How had this whole interchange become more than a thank-you? Could Ashley be right? Had she and Burke been flirting with each other? She had rules in place, damn it. Rules to protect her heart, to protect her family, to keep herself from making the same mistakes she'd made with Aaron. She needed structure. She needed boundaries. Was she falling for this man?

Hazel jerked her hand away, putting the brakes on that possibility. "Excuse me. I'm sorry." Though what, exactly, she was apologizing for, she wasn't certain. Was she leading him on? Making him think that a relationship could happen between them? Did Jedediah want that? Did she?

"Haze—"

But she shook her head, turned and hurried down the hallway after Polly. "I'm sorry."

Hazel clutched her shoulder bag to her chest and followed Polly to the employee locker room at the end of the hall. She did not want to be one of those women who used a man when she needed one, then set him aside. How would that be any different from the way Aaron had treated their marriage? She had no intention of stringing Jedediah along, letting him think he had a chance for something more with her when she couldn't guarantee that was what she wanted, too. Hurting him would be worse than never allowing a serious relationship to happen. Jedediah deserved better than that from her. And she needed to set a better example of an honest relationship for her daughters.

Vowing to have a serious conversation with Jedediah about her rules, once her nerves were a little less frayed by bombs and threats, Hazel caught the door to the locker room before it swung shut. She had her game face back on by the time she stepped inside— even if that air of cool, calm, we've-got-nothing-to-worry-about Mom face was only a facade.

Hazel spotted Polly heading down the center aisle alongside the bench that ran between the rows of lockers. "Knock, knock. Is it okay if I come in?"

Polly waved her into the room. "Sure, Mom."

Nodding to two staff members who were chatting at the front end of the bench, Hazel walked past them. Polly was standing at her open locker door when Hazel wound an arm around her and hugged her to her side. "Hey, young lady. How are you holding up?"

Polly's shoulders lifted with a heavy sigh. "Honestly?"

"Always."

Polly's green eyes darted over to meet hers. "I'm exhausted. This was already a long day without your troubles spilling over into my life." She reached around to share the hug, easing the stinging guilt from her words. "Sorry. That didn't come out right. I don't blame you for any of this. I've just been so worried about you that I didn't realize I needed to be worried about me, too." She smiled as she pulled away and went back to changing out of her scrubs into jeans and a T-shirt. "I'm not looking forward to spending my day off tomorrow dealing with insurance."

"I can help you if you need me to."

Polly tapped her chest with her thumb, asserting her independence. "Grown-up, Mom."

Hazel tapped her own chest, reminding her daughter that some things would never change. "Mother, Polly."

She sat on the bench while Polly exchanged her clogs for a pair of running shoes. She picked up her daughter's discarded scrubs and rolled them up. She wasn't sure what prompted her to dip her nose to the wrinkled bundle and sniff. She inhaled the subtle scents of Polly's shower gel, and the disinfectants and unguents she'd come into contact with throughout the day. Hazel frowned, though, when she realized those were the only scents she was picking up. Was it stereotyping of her to think that a man who lived on the streets would have transferred some sort of pungent odor to her daughter's clothes?

"Don't worry." Polly plucked the bundle from Hazel's hands and tucked them into her backpack. "Laundry is on my to-do list tonight."

"It's not that." Hazel asked the question that had been worrying her. "Now that I'm paranoid about all the men who encounter my family, I was wondering… who was that man who hugged you?"

"Russell?" Polly pulled her ponytail from the back of her T-shirt and studied her reflection in the small mirror inside her locker door. "He's one of the homeless guys my class is volunteering with. They come to the hospital and we practice routine medical care, or we assist the doctors or senior nurses if they have something more serious to deal with. Tonight gave

Russell a dry place to go to get out of this rain, too. He's usually at the Yankee Hill Road shelter, but that's several blocks from here." She muttered a euphemistic curse. "I forgot to ask if he had money for the bus."

"At least it's not chilly tonight," Hazel pointed out. "If he gets wet, he won't catch a cold."

"I'm sure you're right." Polly reached onto the top shelf of her locker. "He reminds me of somebody's grandpa. He said he missed working with me tonight. By the time I got to the area where the group meets, the others were gone. But he waited for me. He heard what happened and could tell I was upset." She pulled out a small rectangle of cardboard and handed it to her. "He gave me this card. Isn't that sweet?"

Hazel supposed she didn't need to worry about a grandfatherly patient paying attention to her daughter. She was the one with the unwanted suitor who was proving to be a threat to them all. Besides, a man who had to resort to crayons and cutting off the front of another card to glue to a piece of cardboard probably didn't have the budget to purchase C-4 and pay for the postage her stalker had already spent on her.

Smiling fondly, Polly sat down to tie her shoes. "Even in Russell's circumstances, he was thinking of me."

Hazel turned the card over to read the message scrawled in three different colors of crayon. *Out of all the people in the world, you're the one I'm thinking of today. Sorry about your car. Russell D.*

"Out of all the people in the world, huh? Your father used to say gushy stuff like that to me when he wanted to apologize for whatever event he forgot or promise he had to break." A message that had usually been accompanied by flowers or a gift they couldn't afford. She'd have preferred a considerate heads-up beforehand if he wasn't going to be at one of Ashley's concerts or plays, or one of Polly's games.

Too many grand gestures and not enough substance and reliability had slowly eroded her trust in Aaron until the girls were the only reason she kept fighting for her marriage. In the end, she'd finally admitted there was nothing left to fight for. And after the night of the accident that was no accident… Leaving with Ashley and Polly had been the best way to protect them from the backlash of Aaron's crimes. Erasing Aaron from her life had been the only way to stop the hateful, then pleading letters from prison. By the time he'd accepted his fate and started writing to Ashley and Polly instead, the girls were too afraid or too disinterested to rebuild a relationship with their father.

Polly bumped her shoulder against hers, cajoling her out of those negative memories. "Hey. I know where your head's at. This isn't Dad we're talking about. Russell loses points for creativity, but I believe the sentiment is legit."

Hazel laced her fingers together with Polly's and squeezed her hand. "You're absolutely right. It's the thought that counts."

"I suppose it's hard to form bonds with people when you're in a situation like Russell's. But I think he looks forward to me checking his blood pressure every week." Polly returned the card to the top shelf of her locker. "That means I'm making a difference in someone's life, right?"

Smiling, Hazel rose to hug her to her side again. "You've been making a difference from the day you were born, sweetie. I don't think there's a puppy, bug or baby bird you didn't want to rescue when you were little."

Polly scrunched her face into a frown. "Funny. I'm not so keen on the bugs now."

"Can anyone join this party?" Ashley beamed a smile as Hazel leaned into her older daughter to include her in the group hug. "It's good to see you laughing again, Mom."

Hazel's mood had lightened considerably from the gloom and suspicion she'd come into the hospital with. "It feels good," she admitted. "Spending time with my two favorite people always makes me feel better. Are you sure you're both okay?"

"The Cooper women have weathered everything else life has thrown at us. We'll get through this, too. Cooper Power."

"Cooper Power," Polly echoed, trading a fist bump with her sister.

Hazel marveled at the bond these two shared. No matter what she accomplished in her life, she knew raising these two fine young women would always be her greatest achievement.

As Polly grabbed her jacket from her locker, Ashley pulled a business card from her purse. "It's not a new car, but I have a present for you, sis."

"A present?" Polly took the business card and flipped it over to read it.

"Sergeant Burke's card with all his numbers." Ashley pulled a second one from her purse to show she'd gotten one, too. "He said to call if we needed anything—whether he's on duty or at home. Even if we just need someone to walk us to our car at night, or we get a flat tire somewhere." She grinned at her sister. "Not that you're going to get a flat tire anytime soon."

"Way to rub it in, dork." Polly stuffed the card into her pocket. "That's awfully nice of the sergeant."

It was. Even without a word or a touch, Jedediah Burke was working his way past Hazel's defenses. His caring offer to her girls warmed her heart and gave her one more reason to toss aside her rules and embrace the possibility of a new relationship.

Ashley slipped her card back into her bag. "He said I could call him Burke. Most of his friends call him that."

"Is that right?" The daughters exchanged a meaningful look before Polly asked, "What do you call him, Mom?"

Apparently, she was going with *Jedediah* now. But somehow, sharing that—even with her daughters—felt like betraying some sort of intimate secret.

"Don't think I don't see what you two are up to. Burke is a good man. We owe him big-time for all the help he's given us. I'm touched that he would extend his protection to you, too."

"He's protecting you? Ooh." Ashley clapped her hands together. "Like a bodyguard? Or a boyfriend?"

Hazel groaned. "I came back here to see if you were all right. Clearly, you are, if you have time to worry about my love life."

"Or lack thereof," Ashley pointed out.

"Stop it." Hazel pointed a stern maternal finger at each of them. "I want you both to come stay with me. There's plenty of room at the condo. Keep us all together until this guy is caught and no one else can get hurt."

"Stay with you?" Ashley frowned before turning her head toward the locker room door as the two women who'd been chatting earlier opened it wide to leave, giving them all a glimpse of the muscular man waiting out in the hallway with two dogs at his side. Burke was leaning against the wall, studying something on his phone, somehow looking both tired and alert as he formed a protective wall between her little family and the outside world that wanted to hurt them. "What if you're entertaining guests?"

Hazel's eyes lingered on his weary expression as the door slowly closed on him. "One, I am not entertaining Burke or any other man. And two, you and Ashley will always come first, even if there was a man in my life."

She was still watching the last glimpse of Burke and wondering what he did to relax after long days like this, or who he leaned on when he needed a boost of support, when Polly squeezed her hand. "When are you going to put yourself first, Mom? Ashley and I are adults now. Don't use us as an excuse to not move on with your life and find happiness."

"Be smart and find it with *him*," Ashley urged. "Burke's a silver fox. You know what that means, don't you?"

"Yes, I know the term. I'm your mother, not dead."

Ashley grinned. "So, you *do* think he's hot."

That was a given.

"I liked it better when I could send you two to your room." Hazel shook her head, forcing herself to remember that the strength she'd imbued in her daughters was there for a reason. "All right. I'll try not to be so much of a mother hen. But don't forget that this guy is no joke. I want you two to look out for each other."

"We will," Polly promised.

"Keep a watchful eye out for anyone paying too much attention to you. Don't go anyplace by yourself. Lock your doors. You know the safety drill. Call me or the police if anything seems wrong to you. Whatever this man wants from me, I am not going to let it hurt my daughters."

Ashley hugged her taller sister to her side. "I'll keep an eye on her, Mom." She tilted her chin up to Polly. "I've got a date tonight with Joe. Maybe we can double. I'm sure he has a friend."

"No, thank you." Polly pulled away to heft her backpack onto her shoulder and close her locker. "I need to study."

"Who's Joe?" Hazel asked. She knew that wasn't the let's-get-married guy Ashley had dumped. The idea of a stranger entering their lives right now worried her. "That's who you were on the phone with?"

"Uh-huh. He's the guy I met a couple of Fridays ago when I went to Fontella's bachelorette party at The Pickle up by City Market."

"The Pickle?" Hazel frowned.

"It's a rooftop bar with pickleball courts. He's a bouncer there. I told you, didn't I?"

She knew about her college friend's wedding, but not the new boyfriend. "No, you didn't."

"He's cool, Mom," Polly volunteered. "I met him when he picked up Ash for the movie last weekend. He's got more tats than any guy I've ever met. But he was funny and super nice. Don't judge a book by its cover and all that."

Bouncer? Tats? Funny and nice? Her daughters really *had* grown up. "Do I get to meet this guy?"

"Do you mind if I invite him to the apartment, then?" Ashley asked Polly, pulling out her phone, ignoring Hazel's question. "We could order a couple of pizzas, and then Joe and I can watch a movie while you're in your room with your books and headphones being all nerdy."

Polly rolled her eyes before shrugging. "That sounds fine. Then none of us will be alone." She nodded toward the exit door, indicating the man waiting patiently on the other side. "Right, Mom?"

Hazel put her hands up in surrender before pulling each daughter in for a hug. "I guess I'm outvoted. Just be safe. And check in with me tomorrow if I don't see you so I know you're all right."

"We will. Love you." Ashley tightened the hug before pulling back and nodding toward the hallway.

"Burke's tired. Hungry, too, I imagine." She gave Hazel a little nudge. "Go. Feed him. He needs some attention."

"He's a grown man." Hazel was arguing against the pull of empathy she'd just been feeling. "He can take care of himself."

Polly took a more logical approach to the relentless matchmaking. "He's been with you all day long. It's after nine o'clock and neither one of you have eaten dinner. Wouldn't that be a nice way to say thank you to him for being such a rock for us today?"

"It's what a good friend would do," Ashley added. She touched her lips. "Although, every man likes a little pretty. Some lip gloss wouldn't hurt."

"Enough with the lip gloss." Hazel tried to stare them down but quickly realized the tactic that had worked to silence an argument when they were children wasn't going to work tonight. Besides, they did have a point. "Fine. I do owe him for his help today." She reluctantly took the lip gloss Ashley offered and dabbed a little color and shine onto her dry lips before pushing it back into her daughter's hand. But she grabbed onto Ashley's fingers and squeezed, still determined they understood her point. "You two know you can't will a relationship to happen between Burke and me just because it amuses you or you think I'm going to wind up alone and living in your spare bedroom. I'm in a good place on my own. I'm happy with my life— except for that idiot who won't leave us alone. I'm more worried about our safety right now than about falling in love again."

"Did she say *falling in love*?" Polly pointed out to her sister.

"That's what I heard. She likes him. She just won't admit it." Ashley was grinning from ear to ear now. "I can see if Joe has a friend he could hook you up with, if that's more of the kind of guy you like."

Another bouncer with tats who was probably half her age? No, thanks.

Polly linked her arm through hers and turned her toward the door. "Mom…there's nothing wrong with being deliriously happy and falling in love again. If you find the right man. And I can't see any way that Sergeant Burke would be the mistake that Dad was."

But what if *she* was the mistake? What if *she* was the one with the rotten judgment who could be tricked into another unhealthy relationship?

Although their hearts were in the right place, her daughters didn't know every detail of the hell Aaron Cooper had put them through. But she did. They thought they were helping by pushing her toward Burke—and they wouldn't let it drop until she gave in and proved them wrong.

Hazel sighed in surrender and traded one more hug before pushing the door open and marching into the hallway. "Call me when you two get home." Burke immediately tucked his phone into his pocket and straightened away from the wall. Barely breaking stride, she grabbed his hand as she passed by and tugged him toward the lobby. "Come with me."

He ordered the dogs into step beside him before

subtly changing his grip on hers, linking their fingers together in a more mutual grasp. "Everything okay?"

"If you call two buttinsky daughters who don't know when to mind their own business okay, then yes, everything's fine."

He halted, pulling her to a stop without releasing her hand. "Did I miss something?"

Hazel glanced up. She couldn't help but smile a reassurance to ease the questioning frown that lined his eyes. "Never mind. Unless you have a better offer, I'm taking you to dinner."

Chapter Five

A better offer? Burke had been waiting for an invitation from Hazel Cooper for a long time. And even though there'd been no declaration of affection, or even an admission that this crazy lust he felt was mutual, getting an invitation to the fourth-floor loft in Kansas City's downtown Library District that Hazel called home felt like taking their relationship to the next level.

By mutual agreement, dinner had ended up being takeout from a burger joint they'd passed on their way from the vet clinic, where she'd picked up her truck and he'd followed her home. He'd been lucky enough to find a place to park on the street a couple of blocks from her building after she'd parked in the gated garage on the street level of the renovated tool and die shop and warehouse. The short walk to join her at the caged-in entrance where she let him in gave Gunny time to do his business before they took the elevator up to the fourth floor.

With only two condos on each floor, Hazel's place felt open and roomy, especially with the wall of floor-to-ceiling windows facing the skyline to the west. He was surprised to see how much of the industrial design of the original building had been preserved in the open ductwork and stained brick walls from when the building had been a hub of manufacturing and commerce near the Missouri River. Although a pair of bedrooms and two bathrooms had been closed in with modern walls, the rest of the loft felt big enough for him to relax in.

Hazel kicked off her shoes the moment she stepped through the front door, fed Cleo and Gunny, and found an old blanket for his dog to sleep on beside the sofa where the smaller dog had curled up. Then she invited him to sit on one of the stools at the kitchen island while she pulled a couple of cold beers from the fridge and set out plates and cloth napkins to make the paper-wrapped sandwiches and fries feel like a real sit-down meal. They talked about the decidedly feminine touches of color and cushy furniture that softened the industrial vibe of the place, her older daughter's apparent obsession with lip gloss that seemed to be part of some joke he didn't understand and her concern about her younger daughter shopping for a new car.

Burke insisted she sit while he cleared the dishes and loaded the dishwasher, offering to go car shopping with Polly. They talked about the rain forcing him to change his training schedule with his officers and their dogs, Royals baseball and whether she preferred the scruffy look he was sporting at 11:00 p.m. to being clean-shaven like when he reported for his shift in the morning. They talked about any- and everything except the bombs, the love letters and the threat she was facing from her unknown stalker.

He decided he liked Hazel's lips, whether they were shiny with gloss, pursed in a bow as she sipped her beer, stretched out in a smile or moving with easy precision as she articulated her words. And though he enjoyed the feeling of intimacy that sharing comfortable spaces and late-night conversation with a beautiful woman gave him, he didn't like that she was avoiding the reason why he and Gunny were here in the first place. He'd always admired Hazel's strength—raising her daughters alone, running her business, caring for others and standing by that strict code of right and wrong she believed in.

But surely, she'd let go sometime. Hazel knew she didn't have to entertain him, right? She didn't have to laugh at his lame teasing or make sure he got that third scoop of ice cream in the sundaes she fixed for dessert. He'd given her apartment the once-over, checking the fire escape and window locks, ensuring the lock on her front door was properly installed, closing the sheer curtains across her living room windows to keep prying eyes from seeing in as she turned on the lights. His offer of security was a given. But he was also here to give her a safety net to drop her guard and give in to the fear and fatigue or whatever she must be feeling.

He closed the dishwasher and turned to face her across the island, catching a glimpse of the big yawn she tried to hide behind the caramel sauce she was licking off her spoon as she finished her sundae. He imagined the swipe of that tongue across his own lips and shifted at the instant stab of heat that tightened his groin and made his pulse race. Man, she had a beautiful mouth. It was getting harder and harder for him to ignore this longing, this sense of rightness he felt every time he spent even a moment with Hazel Cooper. He was 99 percent sure she felt it, too, given the darting glances he spied when she thought his back was turned. But damn that strength of hers. Even as he admired what made her so attractive, he cursed her ability to ignore the possibilities between them.

"Sorry," she apologized around the last bite of the homemade sauce. "It's not the company, I swear."

"Leave something for the dishwasher to do." Burke grinned as he reached across the island to pluck the spoon from her fingers and pick up the empty bowl. He rinsed them off and added them to the dishwasher, carefully choosing his words before he faced her again. "You *do* know that I'm here for you if you need help with anything. An ear to listen. A shoulder to lean on. Someone to watch the place while you crash for a few hours." He braced his hands on the granite countertop and leaned toward her. "You've been through a lot today. Trust me to have your back. Let me take care of you a little bit while you let down your hair and relax or do whatever you need to do to regroup."

She flicked at the silvery blond bangs that played up the mossy green color of her eyes. "What hair?"

Fine. Make a joke out of his caring. He'd better

leave before he argued that he admired how practical her super short hair was, and how it gave him a clear glimpse of the delicate shells of her ears that he wanted to touch and taste. Scrubbing his hand across his jaw, he pushed away from the counter and strode to the back of the couch, where he'd left his ball cap and Gunny's lead. "I guess that's my cue. You don't need me anymore, so I'd better get Gunny home." Even before he gave the command, the big dog was on his feet. "Gunny, *hier.*"

He plunked his hat onto his head and hooked Gunny's lead to his harness.

"Burke." Hazel's stool scudded across the wood planks of the floor. Her bare feet made no sound, but he inhaled the familiar tropical scent of coconut from her soap and shampoo before he heard her behind him. "Jedediah." His muscles jerked beneath the firm grip of her hand on his arm, asking him to stop. Her face was tipped up to his when he glanced down over the jut of his shoulder. Her eyes were weary and worried and sincere. "I'm sorry. I don't mean to make light of your feelings. I'm just not sure I'm prepared to deal with them. Or mine. Not tonight."

He curled his fingers over hers, holding her hand against his skin as he turned. "You don't have to apologize," he conceded. "There was a lot more conversation going on in my head than what came out. You and I are so close, Haze, I sometimes forget that you don't want the same thing between us that I do."

"That isn't necessarily true."

He narrowed his eyes, studying her as she paused

for a moment. What exactly was she saying here? His nostrils flared as he drew in a deep breath, willing himself to be patient and let her speak when everything in him wanted to pounce on that ember of hope she'd just given him. He missed the touch of her hand when she released him to hug her arms around her middle. But her gaze stayed locked on his, and she didn't back away.

"Maybe I've been on my own for so long that I've forgotten how to open up and be in a relationship…" She shrugged, the gesture reminding him that, other than removing her shoes and socks, she still wore the scrubs she'd had on all day. She had to be running on fumes. And yet she was still going to push through her fatigue and finish this conversation. "I know *friendship* doesn't truly explain who we are to each other. But…" She shook her head and smiled without finishing that sentence. "Thank you for looking out for me today. For looking out for Ash and Polly—giving them your cards. It comforted them knowing there was someone they could depend on besides their mother—and that was a comfort to me."

"Sitz." Gunny dropped onto his haunches beside him, his tongue lolling out between his teeth as he waited patiently for a more interesting command. Burke fished into the pocket on his utility vest and handed Hazel a business card, as well. "Here." He slipped the card into her agile, unadorned hand, hating that he could get turned on by even the subtle movement of her fingers brushing against his. "Same

promise I made to them. You call or text me anytime. Day or night. On duty or off. I will be there for you."

"I know. This makes me feel as safe as one of your hugs. And trust me, I love those." She braced her hand against his shoulder and stretched up on tiptoes to kiss his cheek. "Thank you."

As she dropped back to her heels, she drew her fingertips across the scruff of his beard. His pulse beat wildly beneath the lingering caress along his jaw. She had to feel what her touch did to him. "I may change my mind about this scruff. There's just enough silver sprinkled there to remind me of a wolf." Her breath gusted against his neck, as if she was feeling the same rise in temperature he was. "Like the alpha wolf." She gently scraped her short nails against the nap of his stubble again, and the blood pounding through his veins charged straight to his groin. Her eyes narrowed as she processed an unexpected revelation. "You're the alpha of your KCPD pack, aren't you?"

You don't want the same thing between us that I do. That isn't necessarily true.

Yeah. She felt it, too.

How the hell was he supposed to remain some celibate saint of a hero when she touched him like this?

When her surprised gaze darted back to his, Burke lowered his head and pressed his mouth against hers. Although he half expected her to resist, her lips parted to welcome him. She flattened her palm against his cheek and jaw, moaning into his mouth as he gently claimed her. He sampled the shape and softness of her lush bottom lip with a stroke of his tongue before pulling it between his lips. Hazel gave a slight shake of her head. But, just as he hesitated, he realized she wasn't saying no to the kiss. Instead, she was rubbing her mouth against him, seeming to enjoy the texture of his alpha-wolf scruff against her tender skin, or whatever that silly metaphor meant to her. He translated the words into *I think you're irresistibly hot, too*, and let her kiss whatever she wanted, reveling in the same tinder-like friction kindling between them.

He felt her leaning into him, rising onto her toes to take this sensuous investigation to the next level. Burke brought his hands up to frame her face, his fingertips curling beneath those delicate ears to cup the nape of her neck.

She reached up to push his hat off and rubbed her hands against his hair. Burke smiled at her newfound fascination with exploring him and set out on a journey of his own, peppering kisses along her jaw until he found the warm beat of her pulse beneath her ear. Hazel tipped her head back, arching her neck to give him access to sup there. Her bare toes curled atop the instep of his boot and he felt the imprint of proud nipples pressing into his chest as she struggled to get closer. Burke obliged by sliding one hand down over the curve of her hip to cup her sweet, round bottom and lift her onto the desire straining behind his zipper. Her arms settled around his shoulders and she held on, twisting to bring her mouth back to his.

But he'd waited a damn long time for this kiss to happen, and he hadn't satisfied his fantasy of nibbling on her ear and running his teeth against the simple gold stud on her lobe, savoring the contrast between hard and soft that was symbolic of everything about her.

"How long have we been puttin' this off?" he breathed against her ear, loving how she trembled beneath the whisper of air and brush of his lips. Her fingers clutched in the layers of cotton and mesh, digging into the skin and muscle underneath. He wished he'd taken the time to shed his utility vest or her shirt or both before starting this kiss. "I'm tired of pretending we don't want to taste each other—don't want to hold on to each other like—"

"Enough talking." She palmed his jaw in a desperate grasp. "Just—" He captured her mouth in another kiss, spearing his tongue between her lips, tasting sweet caramel and cool cream, and a flavor that was uniquely hers.

Her sigh of surrender told him he'd given her exactly what she wanted.

Burke fell back against the steel door, taking her full weight and loving every curve that flattened against his body, which had been starving for the feel of her. Her feet left the floor entirely as she tightened her arms around his shoulders and pulled herself into the next kiss.

The friction between their bodies created shockwaves that cascaded through him, triggering a snarling groan of need from deep in his chest. "God, how I've wanted you. How I wanted this."

"Do you know how many years have passed since I've been with someone…since I even let myself think about…kissing…" She might be out of practice, but she hadn't forgotten a damn thing about what turned him on. She was eager to touch, raking her fingers across his short hair, down the column of his neck, across his shoulders. They bumped noses and stumbled as he repositioned her in his arms. She smiled and went right back to dragging her teeth along his jawline. "It's been so long since I… I don't remember how to satisfy this itch that's screaming inside me." She laughed against his mouth. "Much less yours. I might need a refresher course."

"You'll get no complaints from me."

"But—"

"Enough talking," he teased. The tips of his fingers caught in her hair as he framed her face between his hands, guiding her mouth back to his. "It's okay, babe. I want this, too. I can't believe this is finally—"

"Babe?" She broke off the kiss, going still in his arms, repeating the single word as if it was a curse. Hazel braced her hands against his shoulders and blinked him into focus, as if she was coming to after being lost in a dream. Maybe he'd been dreaming, too, thinking that they'd turned a corner in their relationship. Before he could even catch his breath, she released her grip on him and slid her feet back to the floor.

"Guess I got a little carried away." He straightened away from the door, drawing her back into his arms. "Making out like a man half my age isn't usually my style. Guess I've been savin' up." Despite the joke, he silently vowed to dial it back a notch before he went too far and scared her away.

But, apparently, he already had.

Hazel palmed his chest and pushed him back. "What did you call me?"

Any illusion of dream time was done. Burke shook his head, clearing the lingering confusion from his thoughts. "I don't know. *Babe?* I can do *honey* or *sweetheart* if you prefer—"

"No." She was vaguely staring at the middle of his chest where her hand rested, replaying the last couple of minutes in her head, too. "Don't call me that. Don't call me any of that."

At least she had the courtesy to struggle to soothe her erratic breathing, just like he was fighting to inhale a steady, normal breath. She couldn't lie and say that kiss hadn't affected her, too. "Okay. I won't…" He clasped her shoulders to rub his hands up and down her arms until he could think with his brain again. "We can go slow."

"Burke…" She shrugged off his grasp. Her gaze locked firmly onto his. "Jedediah. We have to stop. We aren't a pair of hormone-fueled teenagers. We're old enough to know better than to give in to our urges. We're both exhausted. We're not thinking straight."

"I am. I'm not second-guessin' any of this." He reached for her again, hoping to ease her doubts, but she strong-armed him out of her personal space.

"Stop."

"Because I called you *babe*?" Burke held both hands out in surrender, understanding her right to end any contact she wasn't comfortable with, even if he didn't fully understand why.

The faint lines beside her eyes deepened with an apology. "That's what Aaron called me."

Swearing one choice word, Burke rubbed his hand across his spiky hair. "How was I supposed to know? I'm sorry I upset you." He could feel the short-circuited desire still sparking through his fingertips. But instead of reaching for her, he bent down to retrieve his KCPD ball cap from the floor beside Gunny. "Guess I ruined the moment, huh?"

Despite his fatigue, every muscle in him was tight with desire. That kiss had been pure heaven. And it had only primed the fuel burning inside him. He wanted more with Hazel Cooper. He wanted the right to kiss her every time he walked away from her. Hell. He didn't want to walk away. He wanted to stay the night. Feel those cute, naked toes running up his leg and her body melting into his as she surrendered to his kisses.

"I'm not blaming you. But it's the wake-up call I needed to remind myself that I have rules. I don't do relationships. I don't want to—not with you."

He heard that message like a slap across the face. He pulled his cap onto his head and reached for Gunny's leash. "That's clear enough."

Hazel's fingers fisted in his vest, stopping him from turning to the door. "Not because I'm not tempted to see where you and I might go...but... because I *am* tempted. I've ignored the attraction between us because I don't want to risk what we have. I don't want to lose you from my life."

Why did the possibility of everything she'd just admitted make her look so sad?

He captured her hand against his heart. "Let me get this straight—you're willing to throw away a chance at us becoming more than friends because you're scared it could be really incredible between us?"

"What if it isn't? I'll admit it—I haven't been with a man in years. And I miss that. But what if this is just chemistry that flares out once we give in and get it out of our system? Or we're two lonely people who are so desperate to make an intimate connection that we're jumping on feelings that aren't really there? Think how that could taint what we already have." She tapped his chest with every sentence. "What I know is real. What I know is good and special."

Real. Good. Special. Sounded like a perfect scenario to him. "The best marriages I know are when the man and woman are friends first. That doesn't mean there's no passion. No soul-deep connection that defies logic. All of that goes into a relationship."

"Marriage? That's quite a jump from our first kiss to exchanging rings." Hazel pulled away, finally putting some distance between them. "You've been divorced a long time, Burke. Are you sure you can do a serious committed relationship? That you even want that?"

Back to *Burke*, huh? Boy, when she pushed him away, she pushed hard. "After Shannon, I never found the right woman I could put that much faith in—until

I met you. I've wanted you for years, and in all that time, until this past week, until tonight, you've kept me at arm's length. But I'm still here. I think that shows a pretty solid commitment." After a moment she nodded, at least giving him that. "You've been divorced a long time, too. Maybe you're the one who's afraid to commit."

"Guilty as charged. But I have my reasons."

"I know you do. But, Haze, when your heart's involved, there's always a risk. You're sure you're not just afraid of getting hurt?"

"Why? You gonna hurt me?" She tried to make it a joke, but neither of them laughed. "I know you wouldn't mean to. But the last time I followed my heart, I nearly died. I can't afford to be impulsive again."

"What?" Her marriage had dissolved years before the two of them had met. And though her ex-husband's crimes had been big news in Kansas City, he'd been on active duty back then, stationed overseas, and had never heard all the details. Once he'd gotten to know the woman Hazel was now, he hadn't cared who she or her ex had once been. In his recent research into her ex's criminal history, he'd seen the charge of attempted murder along with the fraud and embezzlement charges. But he had no idea who her husband's intended victim had been.

A cold feeling of dread crept down Burke's spine. "What do you mean *died*?"

Chapter Six

"It's a long story, and I'm too tired to get into all of it tonight." The chill Burke felt must be contagious. Hazel crossed to the back of the couch, where she'd shed her scrubs jacket and pulled it on over her T-shirt and jeans. "I stood by Aaron like a good wife when I found out how he'd cheated all those people out of their investments and retirement funds. Gave him the benefit of the doubt. Hoped someone else was responsible and he was the scapegoat who'd been falsely accused."

"I've heard he put you through hell," Burke conceded. "What does that have to do with us?"

She paced over to the curtains and pulled one aside to stare out into the moonless night dotted with the lights of downtown KC. "Even after Aaron was arrested and the DA was hounding me to testify against him, I did everything I could to make our marriage work. Ashley and Polly were six and four. They didn't understand what was going on around them—why friends suddenly stopped calling, why kids were mean to Ashley in school."

Burke swore. "I had no idea it was that bad."

"I did everything I could to try to keep things as normal as possible for them—to keep our family intact. I gave up my life savings, my self-worth, my happiness and any sense of security because I thought it was the right thing to do. I thought love was going to conquer all." Hazel released the curtain and faced him. "It didn't." She hugged herself around her middle, and every cell in his body begged for the right to cross the room and pull her into his arms to share his warmth and strength. "I've worked hard for a long time to regain everything I lost. I don't know if I'm willing to risk that again."

"You haven't regained everything," he pointed out sadly. "You don't trust your own judgment. You don't trust your heart."

Sad green eyes locked on to his, and she nodded her agreement. "I paid a heavy price for loving Aaron."

To keep himself by the door, Burke reached down to pet Gunny's flanks. Like him, the working dog was getting antsy about staying in place instead of taking action. But Hazel needed to talk. "We all make mistakes, Doc. Hell, I've made my share. We're allowed to learn from them and move on. Mistakes don't mean we don't get to be happy."

"I get the learning part. Most people's mistakes aren't as big as the one I made in marrying Aaron."

He vowed then and there to request Aaron Cooper's case file and court transcripts and read them down to the very last detail. He had a sick feeling there was still more to this story, and he wished Hazel trusted him enough to tell him the worst. But she was locking down tight, letting him know he wasn't getting the answers he needed tonight.

"You can't judge every man by your ex's standard. I'm not like him, and you know it. I would never ask you to change who you need to be. And I'd be pissed if you thought you had to." Gunny whined an empathetic protest and Cleo popped up on the back of the couch to see what was upsetting her friend. "I'm a patient man, but you keep making me work too hard, and I might quit trying."

Hazel scooped up the one-eyed schnauzer and hugged the dog to her chest as she joined him at the door again. "That makes it sound like I've been leading you on. I swear, that's not my intention. That's why I never should have kissed you."

"I know you don't want to hurt me. Don't add that guilt on top of everything else you're dealing with. Your honesty is one of those things that make me want to be with you. Still, it's not fair of me to push when you're vulnerable like this." He scrubbed his fingers around Cleo's ears, glad that Hazel would at least accept comfort from her dog if not from him. "If it makes any difference, you don't have the monopoly on being gun-shy about risking everything on a new relationship. Sticking with you is a risk for me, too. I don't relish failing again."

"You didn't fail," she said, and he couldn't miss how her expression changed to one of unflinching support the moment he shared his own weakness. "When we first became friends, you said your wife cheated on you while you were deployed. That's hardly your fault."

For him, for everyone else, Hazel was a warrior. Why couldn't she put that fight into her own happiness? Did she really believe they were destined to fail if they gave in to their deepest feelings?

"I guess our bond wasn't strong enough for Shannon to be without me 24-7. I must not inspire that kind of loyalty. Not with her—and apparently, not with you."

"Of course you do. Look at the men and women you work with, the dogs you train. Look at us. That loyalty—that unquestioning trust—those are the very things I don't want to jeopardize."

"You can have both—friendship *and* love." He gave up on petting the dog and brushed his fingertip along Hazel's jaw. "If you trust me to be your friend, then why can't you trust me to love you?"

"I won't risk my emotional security for a roll in the hay or a chance at temporary bliss when it all might end in heartache and you walking out of my life."

"Who says I'm offering you a roll in the hay?" he teased, despite the evidence that had pushed against the seam of his BDU a few minutes earlier.

"I'm cautious, not blind." Her gaze dropped briefly to his crotch. It was good to see her smile again. "Promise me one thing, no matter what happens between us. Never lie to me."

He smiled back. "Deal."

"And I promise to do my damnedest not to give you false hope. Not to hurt you."

To hell with tiptoeing around his feelings. He slipped his hand around to cup the back of her head. Ignoring the dog squished between them, he kissed her squarely on the mouth, stealing her gasp of surprise. He kissed her hard. Kissed her well. Kissed her until she understood he'd never tire of kissing that beautiful, responsive mouth, and pulled away. "*That's* chemistry. It isn't a bad place to start a relationship." He reached behind him to unlock the door. "I've been through a lot of life, Haze. I'm tough. I'm not going to break—or walk away when you need me—because of a few dings to my ego, or because we're in different places in our relationship. Loving you may not be as simple as a fairy tale, but that doesn't mean I'm going to stop."

"Burke—"

He pressed his fingertip to her lips, silencing any more protest. "Good night, Dr. Coop. Lock up behind me."

Burke skipped the elevator and took Gunny down the stairs, knowing they both needed to work off some of the energy pent up inside them. He opened the steel mesh door at the pedestrian exit to the parking garage and waited for it to close and automatically lock behind him before jogging across the street to the parking lot framed by a narrow grassy area and let the dog relieve himself.

While Gunny sniffed and staked out a couple of trees and shrubs in regular dog mode, Burke took note of the young couple arguing over the roof of their car in the parking lot. He dismissed their petty whining as no threat and glanced back at Hazel's building. He tilted his head to the bright lights behind the fourth-floor windows, wondering how his favorite veterinarian was coping with the aftermath of that intense conversation and make-out session, which he'd let get out of hand the moment she'd kissed him back. He shook his head and tugged on Gunny's leash to get them moving toward his truck. He couldn't tell if he was angry or hurt. Probably both. "You handled that well, Sarge. All those years of biding your time and you blow it all in one night."

After the rain they'd had earlier, he expected the night to be cool. Instead, a fog of humidity hung in the air, closing in around him.

What the hell did she mean when she said her marriage to Aaron Cooper had nearly killed her? Could the tragedy of that marriage have anything to do with the creepy love letters and bomb threats? Her ex had been out of prison for almost a year now. Were the threats punishment for divorcing him? And did she have any idea how badly he wanted to protect her from bombs and stalkers and a painful past that still haunted her?

He didn't suppose there was any way to hide his feelings for Hazel now—no way to step back from laying it all out there. He wasn't worried about salvaging his pride—he was old enough to have learned that there were things in life worth a lot more than a man's ego. But he was also old enough to know that love was a precious thing, and that trust was probably the greatest gift a person could give him...and

Hazel had refused to trust his belief that they were meant to be together in every way. He was stumped on how to get her to take that leap of faith with him. And it nagged at him to think that maybe she'd be better off if he didn't even try.

But losing Hazel… The idea of never working side by side with her or trading dumb jokes or kissing her again gutted him.

He exchanged a nod with a trio of young men they passed on the sidewalk before halting at a traffic light. One of the preppie guys in the front waved to someone up the hill behind Burke and rushed on to meet their friend. The one in the hoodie following a few steps behind them ducked his head and hurried after his buddies.

Could Burke be happy with the status quo anymore?

His phone rang in his pocket as the light changed. He led Gunny around the standing water at the curb and pulled his cell from his utility vest. For a split second, his dark mood skyrocketed at the slim hope Hazel had changed her mind. He wisely cooled his jets, though, knowing that at this time of night, even though they were off the clock, it was probably a work call.

"And the night just gets worse," he muttered when he saw the number.

Gunny jerked against his lead, stopping halfway across the street to glance behind them. Burke figured the low-pitched growl was just the dog tracking where the three young men had gone—or maybe he was sensing Burke's response to the name on his cell screen.

His ex-wife, Shannon.

"Gunny, *fuss*." The dog fell into step beside him again. They reached the next curb before he answered the call. "What do you want?"

"Hello to you, too." Her familiar giggle, which he'd once found so charming, grated on his nerves.

If he wasn't a cop, trained to respond to anyone in need—even the woman who'd broken his heart as a younger man—he wouldn't have answered at all. "It's late, Shannon. Is there an emergency? Is Bill all right?"

"You're not at home."

How would she know that? Ah, hell. Instinctively, he glanced around the intersection, wondering if she'd had someone track down his location. Thankfully, there was no sign of her. Had she gone to his house? It was located far enough away on the outskirts of the city that he could have a big fenced-in yard and some mature trees where Gunny could play. A home that was nowhere near the pricey Ward Parkway neighborhood where Shannon and her husband lived. "Are you at my place?"

"I'm parked in your driveway. The lights are out and no one's home." Her breathy sigh, followed by a dramatic sniffle, told him she'd been crying. "I needed to see you."

Burke slowed his pace, feeling a tinge of concern. Maybe there *was* a problem. "Shannon?"

"Why do I have to hear through the grapevine that my husband was nearly killed by a bomb today?"

And poof. Any concern he felt vanished. Now he was just annoyed that she'd dropped by his house unannounced. Gunny tugged on his lead again, curious about something only a dog could see or smell in the shadows. Burke tugged right back, demanding the dog sit and stay beside him. Gunny never ignored a command unless he was off leash. Something had caught the dog's attention, and Burke had been his partner long enough not to ignore his partner's instincts.

He paused on the corner, turning a slow 360 to see if he could spot whatever had the dog's attention. A bar two blocks up had patrons spilling out onto the sidewalk with their drinks and smokes. The rock music was loud, but not illegally so. The arguing couple had driven off, and the trio of young men had disappeared. But they could have gone into the bar, turned a corner or gotten into their vehicle and left downtown. A little farther up the street, a city bus was brightly lit and picking up passengers near one of the big hotels.

Burke kept searching for anything or anyone that would put Gunny on alert. "Don't go all drama queen on me, Shannon. First, it's *ex*-husband, three times removed. Unless you've divorced Bill Bennett and I haven't read about it in the paper yet." The irony that her fourth husband was a divorce attorney wasn't lost on Burke. "And second, which bomb are you talking about?"

"Which...? There was more than one? You and that dog. Why can't you have a regular pet like everybody else?" He could picture her wiping away tears from her dark almond-shaped eyes now that she understood he wasn't swayed by them. "I'm talking about the bomb threat at the veterinary clinic. I saw the report on TV."

He'd been clearing the hospital when the evening newscasts had aired. Maybe a reporter had caught him on camera. "A friend was sent a package at her work. Gunny identified the explosive and we cleared the building. It wasn't really a bomb. Just the parts to make one. I wasn't in any significant danger."

"Significant? But you were in *some* danger. I was right to be worried."

He was a cop. He'd been a soldier before that. The danger surrounding either job was a given. "Go home, Shannon. I'm not yours to worry about."

Although it had been years since he'd come home from a deployment to find her in bed with one of the attorneys she'd worked for as a paralegal, and the anger, heartbreak and blow to his pride had long since mellowed, her betrayal had left a mark that influenced how he approached relationships in the years since. That was probably why it had taken him so long to realize that Hazel was the only woman he wanted to be with, why he'd been content to let things simmer beneath the surface of their relationship...until tonight.

Burke suspected that, in her own way, Shannon truly had loved him, and maybe part of her still did, judging by the infrequent phone calls like this one.

But the infatuation shared by high school sweethearts hadn't lasted. She hadn't been cut out to be a military wife. Even with access to support groups, being alone for extended periods of time, managing the day-to-day responsibilities of running a home, working a job and living a life on her own just weren't in her skill set. Even after he'd retired from the Army and Reserves, he doubted she would have done any better with the hours and dangers of him being a cop, even though he was on home soil.

"That's cold, Jed. You know my heart will always belong to you."

"Don't let Bill hear you say that." Since he hadn't spotted anything unusual to account for Gunny's restlessness, he headed on toward his truck. "I'd hate to be the cause of his own divorce."

"About that… You know I've matured since we were married. We were too young. *I* was too young. I didn't understand about commitment then. And I was so lonely. But now I—"

Beep.

"Hold on a second, I've got an incoming message."

Thank God. He'd been down this road with Shannon too many times before. She must have gotten into an argument with her current husband. Every time she hit a bump in the road with her latest relationship, she got these sentimental urges to call Burke to reconnect—expecting him to fix the issue, comfort her or, *ain't never gonna happen*, even take her back. Hell. Maybe she called all her exes looking for sympathy when the going got rough. He had no interest in a woman he couldn't trust. And knowing Shannon's affairs had led her from one husband to the next told him she wasn't going to change.

Burke pulled up the text and frowned. Hazel's name was at the top of the screen.

I need you. Bring Gunny.

A chill of apprehension trickled down his spine. Burke glanced up at the windows of the old tool and die building. Even from this distance, he could see that all the lights had gone out in Hazel's condo. Every lamp and overhead bulb had been blazing when he left.

"Fuss!" Burke was already moving, jogging, pulling Gunny into a loping run beside him. "Shannon, I have to go."

"Let me guess—work?"

"Goodbye."

"It's another woman, isn't it? You said *her* workplace. Are you seeing someone? It's that doggie doctor, isn't it?" Anger edged into her voice. "You told me she was one of the guys, Jed. She means more to you than that, doesn't she?"

Uh-uh. He wasn't going down that road with her. He wasn't the one who cheated, so she had no right to be jealous, and he wasn't about to feel guilty about answering a friend's call for help. "You should be talking to your husband about whatever's going on, not me. Bye."

"Jed, don't hang—"

He ended the call, texted back an On my way and stuffed the phone into his pocket before lengthening his stride to match Gunny's. In a matter of seconds, they were back at Hazel's building. But the cage that closed in the parking garage and pedestrian access stopped him like a brick wall. He didn't have a key card to swipe or pass code to punch into the access panel beside the door. The fact that there were no more texts to give him any idea of what was going on only ratcheted up his concern.

He quickly typed in Hazel's condo number and pressed the intercom button.

His blood pressure rose with every second of silence before he heard a quiet, hesitant voice. "Burke?"

"It's me, Haze. Are you all right? Let me in."

Gunny barked, adding his voice to the urgent request. The dog was probably picking up on the tension running down the lead from his partner's hand, but it was enough of a confirmation of their identity for Hazel to buzz them in. The lights were on inside, so this wasn't something as benign as a power outage. Hazel was hiding in the dark for a reason. After a quick glance around the lobby, looking for any signs of an intruder, they vaulted up the stairs and knocked on Hazel's door.

"Sergeant Burke, KCPD," he announced, warning anyone who might be a threat on the other side of that door. "Open up."

He heard a yip from Cleo and a muted cry a split second before the dead bolt turned and the door flew open.

Hazel walked straight into his chest, wound her arms around his waist and clung to him as though a tornado might blow her away if she didn't hang on tightly enough. Burke didn't mind the contact one bit. But standing out on the landing, exposed to potentially prying eyes, wasn't the place to do it. He hustled Gunny into the apartment, wrapped an arm around Hazel's trembling shoulders and pushed her inside, kicking the door shut behind him.

"Voran!" He ordered the dog to search the apartment while he held Hazel close and peered into the semidarkness over her head. The only light on in the whole place was the flashlight shining from her cell phone, which sat on the coffee table in front of the sofa. "Anyone here besides you and Cleo?"

Her fingers convulsed beneath his utility vest at the back of his shirt as she shook her head beneath his chin. "I'm sorry. First, I chase you away, and now I can't seem to let go."

"I said you could lean on me." But he needed to know what the problem was first. "What's happened? Why are the lights out?" He spied Gunny moving from one room to the next, with Cleo limping along in his shadow. Surely the small dog would have been making noise if there was someone in here besides his mistress. Gunny cleared the back bedroom and trotted down the hallway toward him to be rewarded with a toss of his ball on a rope. As both dogs took off after the toy, Burke leaned back against Hazel's grip to frame her jaw between his hands and tip her face up to his. Her skin was cool, her cheeks pale. He wanted to punch somebody for rattling her like this. "Haze, you gotta talk to me."

She bravely raised her gaze to his. "He called. Right after you left."

No need to explain who *he* was. "What did he say?"

"Come to the window."

"Tell me what he said first. Did he threaten you?"

"No. That's what he said. That's all he said." Nodding that she was all right enough for now, Hazel took his hand and led him to the curtains. *"Come to the window."*

When she started to open the edge of the first curtain, Burke pulled her behind him and peered outside over the street, parking lot and buildings. Even with the sky covered by clouds, with the streetlamps, the neon signs of the nearby bar and traffic lights, it was brighter outside than it was inside the condo. He saw the same variety of faceless people walking the street and going about their business that he'd seen from the sidewalk below. "What am I looking for?"

"Is he gone?" She tugged on his arm to get to the window. "I just saw… I'm not making this up."

"I know you're not."

"It was him." Hazel drifted away from the window. "In the parking lot across the street. I saw him. Everyone else was going somewhere. But he was just standing there. Looking up at me. His face was weird, like he had some sort of deformity."

"Do you know anyone like that?"

"No. I tried to get him to say something else. I

wanted to know who he was, why he was doing this to me. All I could hear was him breathing. I hung up and texted you. Turned the lights out so he couldn't see me. But he already had."

"Can you describe anything else about him?"

"I couldn't judge his height from this angle, but kind of a beefy build. He had on a dark hoodie. Dark pants. Like the man Polly described at the hospital."

Burke swore, closing the curtain. The man following the preppie boys had worn dark blue pants and a hoodie. He hadn't been one of them. He was... "I saw him. Passed him on the street." Burke had been too distracted by frustration and self-recriminations to piece together what he'd observed earlier. "I never saw his face, but Gunny recognized him. Something about his smell must have been familiar. Or he still had trace explosives on him." Burke pulled the curtain shut with more force than was necessary. "I don't see him out there now."

"He looked right at me. Made a stupid little heart symbol over his chest. Like that would mean something to me. And then he gestured like...boom." She placed her hands on either side of her head, then quickly pulled them away, splaying her fingers. *Head blown.* An all-too-familiar gesture indicating an explosion—a threat meant for Hazel.

"Let me see your phone."

He followed her to the coffee table, where she turned off the flashlight app and pulled up the recent call list. He texted the number to Dispatch and requested a trace, although he'd bet money that the call had come from a burner phone. Then he headed to the door.

"How do I make this stop?" Hazel followed him to the door. "He knows where I live. He knows where I work, who my children are. He has my number..." She caught him by the arm and stopped him. "You're going after him?" The panic fled her voice when she realized his intent. "You said he was gone."

"I said I didn't see him." He squeezed her hand in a subtle reassurance as he pried it from his arm. He had a job to do. She seemed to understand that. Her eyes had lost that wild lack of focus and were trained on him as she nodded. He called Gunny to him and unhooked the shepherd's leash. *"Bleibe."*

"Stay?" Gunny sat squarely on his haunches beside Hazel. "Don't you need him?"

"No." He unsnapped his holster and rested his hand on the butt of his Glock. "He stays with you and protects you, in case this guy has already gotten into the building somehow. What's your entry code?" She gave him the number. "This door stays locked until I get back."

"What if he calls again?"

"Switch phones with me. If that bastard calls, he's going to talk to me."

Hazel handed over her cell and clutched his to her chest. She drifted closer to Gunny and buried her fingers in his fur. "Be careful."

"You, too."

The dead bolt slid into place behind him. Burke made a quick sweep through the building, startling one couple who were enjoying a good-night kiss on the top floor. No hoodie. And though the guy could have easily ditched it somewhere, these two weren't hiding their faces from him. And they both wore jeans. Burke's grim expression and curt command chased them into the apartment. The rest of the building and parking garage were clear of anyone who looked suspicious. Once outside, he moved through the parking lot across the street, checking vehicles and the spaces in between. He entered the bar for a quick once-over and gave the bouncer at the door a brief description of the perp. But there were too many possible suspects who fit the general description for him to make any useful identification. He checked down the street in the other direction. A block farther, and he'd be on an overpass crossing the interstate running through the north end of downtown KC. There was simply too much ground here for one man to cover. Whoever had been terrorizing Hazel was gone.

Burke was jogging back to Hazel's building when her phone beeped with a text. He eyed his surroundings and got no sense of anyone watching him before he pulled it up on the screen. It was a fuzzy picture of Hazel peeking out her window into the night.

Do I have your attention now? I don't expect you to answer. But I do expect you to listen. I want you to know that everything you have belongs to me.

FYI, your policeman and your dog can't stop me from taking what's rightfully mine.

"Hell." Burke ran the last block and typed in the code to enter the building.

By the time he was back at Hazel's, he was worn-out and angry and relieved to see her with color in her cheeks again as she locked the door behind him. He briefly considered trashing the text, so her healthy, confident look wouldn't disappear again. But the cop in him knew he needed to save it as evidence. Making a case against a stalker almost always relied on having a stack of circumstantial evidence that showed a pattern of harassment and escalating danger. Besides, he'd promised to always be honest with her.

"It's decaf." She handed him a mug of coffee she'd brewed while he'd been out. "I used your phone to call the girls. They're fine. They haven't seen anything suspicious at their place." The coffee smelled heavenly and reviving, but he set it aside to capture her gaze. "What is it? What did you find?"

"Nothing. He's gone, or he would have seen me reading this." He handed her the phone. "I doubt he would have kept silent about me interfering with his private conversation with you."

She read the text and went pale again. Without comment, she simply picked up his mug and carried it back to the kitchen, where she lingered at the counter with her back to him. She busied her hands by adding half-and-half to the mug and sipping on the hot brew herself.

"What does he want from me? Revenge? My undying devotion? Is he getting off on toying with me like this?" She stood at the refrigerator door as the flare of emotion ebbed and her shoulders sagged. "I can't tell if he thinks he loves me or he wants to hurt me."

"Maybe both. Obsession can change from one to the other pretty quickly."

She drank another sip of creamy coffee and abruptly changed the subject. "Someone named Shannon called while you were out. I saw her name. Isn't she your ex-wife? She left a voice mail. I hope it wasn't important."

"It wasn't."

Hazel set down her mug with a decisive thunk. "You're going to think I'm an absolute nutcase, but could you—"

"I'm staying."

She turned to find him draping his utility vest over the back of the couch. He knelt to remove Gunny's harness. He ruffled the dog's fur and sent him off to play with his rope ball. "The couch will do just fine."

Her smile told him he'd made the right decision. Not that he was giving her any choice.

"Good." She padded down the hallway and brought him a pillow and covers. She made up the sofa and fluffed the old blanket for Gunny. "I have the extra bedroom I keep for the girls. You could sleep on a real mattress."

Burke removed his gun, belt and badge, and set them on the coffee table within easy reach. "I want to be between you and anything that comes through that front door."

"Are you afraid he'll come back? That he can actually get into the building to get to me?"

"Aren't you?" He could see she was by the bleak shadows in her eyes. Burke took her gently by the shoulders and turned her toward her bedroom. She didn't protest as he dug into the tension cording her neck and followed right behind her. "It's been a long day for both of us. We have work tomorrow. Try to sleep. In the morning, we'll call Detectives Bellamy and Cartwright and fill them in on this latest incident."

She stopped at the bedroom doorway, and they shared a smile at Cleo pawing herself a nest in the middle of Hazel's blanket. "I seem to be saying it a lot lately, but…" Hazel turned and tilted her eyes to his. "Thank you."

"Go to bed, Doc."

"I haven't been scared like this for a long time."

"I know."

"I hate being scared. I'm used to handling whatever I need to on my own."

"I know that, too."

"I'm sorry about arguing with you earlier. It's not that I don't care—"

He silenced her with a finger over her lips. "That was a discussion, not an argument. An honest exchange of what we're thinking and feeling. People who trust like you and me can have those kinds of conversations. It helped me understand those ground rules of yours. It helps me be patient." When she didn't immediately turn in or protest his touch, Burke brushed her bangs across her forehead and cupped the side of her face. "You'll be okay, Doc. You're the strongest woman I know. Gunny and I are just here to back you up."

She considered his words, then stretched up on tiptoe to kiss the corner of his mouth. "Thank you for saying that. It helps me believe it. Good night, Jedediah."

After she closed the door and turned on a light inside, he checked the locks and windows one last time. Once the light had gone out beneath her door, he untied his boots and settled onto the couch, tucking his gun beneath the pillow.

They were back to *Jedediah*. He breathed a sigh that was part fatigue and part relief. He hadn't ruined everything by putting his feelings out on the table. Sure, he wanted more than a peck on the cheek, more than a closed door and distance between them.

But he knew Hazel was safe, and for now, that was enough.

Chapter Seven

"Hey, babe. I know I'm not supposed to contact you, but we need to talk. It's really important."

Hazel knew the first voice mail from her ex today by heart now. And the second. And the fifth.

Her phone vibrated in the pocket of her jeans, stealing her attention away from her current patient, telling her she'd just ignored call number six. How dare Aaron Cooper keep contacting her?

Having her stalker call her last night to taunt her had left her feeling vulnerable and afraid. Waking up to find Jedediah Burke sitting at her kitchen island, drinking from a fresh pot of coffee and reading the news on his phone like he was a normal part of a normal day had gone a long way toward restoring her equilibrium. Not only was Burke a familiar presence, but his strength and easy authority made her feel like there was nothing the world could throw at him that he couldn't handle. And that air of calm confidence made her feel like she could handle it, too.

But that equilibrium that had quickly been knocked off-kilter for a very different reason when she sat beside him with her own mug of coffee. She smelled freshly showered man, felt the warmth radiating off his body and filling the space between them, and found herself silently mourning the sexy salt-and-pepper scruff that had vanished from his clean-shaven jaw this morning.

Burke was one of her best friends.

He was also solid and hot and one hell of a kisser.

For a few minutes last night, she'd been a woman on fire in his arms, intimately aware of every sexy attribute the mature man possessed. Jedediah had done far more than make her feel safe. He'd made her feel desirable, hungry, eager to be alive. After all these years of denying herself, he made her want to be with a man again. It had been empowering to be the woman he couldn't resist. He said he loved her. But did she have it in her to love someone again?

The phone vibrating in her pocket was stark evidence of how wrong choices could ruin so many lives. She already had five messages on her phone today to remind her of those mistakes. The first message had been friendly, polite, even apologetic. But with each call Aaron sounded more and more irritated, more like the desperate, dangerous man he'd become before the divorce.

"Hazel. It's Aaron. Pick up. I have a right to see my girls. You once said you forgave me for what I did to you. I know you won't believe me, but you still mean something to me. And I love my girls. I'm not the man I was sixteen years ago. Prison changed me. You need to let me be a dad to them."

There was a reason for the restraining order against her ex that had been in place for sixteen years. Once a man endangered her children, betrayed her trust and tried to kill her, she really didn't want to hear from him anymore.

A stalker with an explosive hobby.

Jedediah talking love and second chances.

Aaron harassing her with call after call today.

How had her safe, predictable life gotten turned completely upside down like this?

"Dr. Coop?" Todd Mizner's hand closed over her shoulder and Hazel startled. "Sorry. Everything okay?" he asked before pulling away.

She glanced up at the concern in his blue eyes and gave a brief jerk of her head. Time to focus on the problem right here in front of her.

She looked across the stainless-steel examination table into the unblinking scowl from her client, Wade Hanson. For an out-of-shape man who must be in his sixties or early seventies, wearing grungy workman's clothes that had seen better days, he still managed to look intimidating. He had every right to be upset by her lack of concentration on this long, rainy afternoon. The dog he'd brought in needed some serious attention, not a vet who was too distracted by her own problems to provide the care the alarmingly skinny cattle dog mix needed. Of course, Hanson's combative stance with his beefy arms crossed over his potbelly, and his jaw grinding away on the chaw of tobacco in his cheek, could have more to do with the suspicions she hadn't done a very good job of hiding.

"It's not good." She tilted her chin, catching Mr. Hanson studying her from beneath the brim of his soiled ball cap. He quickly shifted his gaze back to the skinny dog on the table while she moved the stethoscope and checked for gut sounds to confirm her initial diagnosis.

"You can fix her, though, right?" Hanson spoke without moving his jaw. Probably a good thing since she didn't want to see the tobacco juice staining his teeth. But he gave her the sense that he was a powder keg about to blow—an unsettling analogy considering recent events. Hazel wondered exactly where that anger seething beneath the surface was directed.

One last vibration on her phone told her Aaron had left another message. Ignoring both the pestering from her ex and the critical glare from Mr. Hanson, she finished her exam. Besides the dog being clearly overbred, she could see ribs and hip bones through the mutt's thin skin and spotted tan fur. A stray scrounging for food on the streets would have more body mass than this poor waif. She had no fever or obvious masses to indicate a serious illness. And Hazel didn't want to draw any blood to check for internal parasites until she'd gotten some intravenous fluids in her to increase her blood volume and stabilize her. "This is a working breed. Athena should be compact, muscular. She needs to be spayed, too. You should have brought her to me sooner." Maybe dropped a few bites of whatever had put that paunch on Hanson's belly to the floor for his pet. "Neglect like this doesn't happen overnight." Since the animal couldn't tell her what she'd suffered, Hazel had to ask the owner questions. "Has she been keeping food down?" She bristled when he didn't immediately answer. "Have you been feeding her?"

Wade scratched at his scraggly white beard and grumbled. "I didn't do it. Margery took her to piss me off. I just got Athena back from her."

Interesting deflection of her queries. Even a few days was too long for this dog to be suffering without basic care. "Your wife did this?"

"Ex-wife. Athena should have been mine when she left. But my selfish, vindictive—"

"I get the picture." Unfortunately, this wasn't the first time Hazel had seen a patient who'd been the victim of an unfriendly split. It wasn't the first time she'd defended the innocent pet who'd been either forgotten or used as a weapon to punish an ex. It was just as likely that Hanson was lying, and he'd taken the dog to spite his ex. Either way, she would see to it that Athena got the help she needed. Hazel set her stethoscope on the counter behind her and slid her arms beneath the dog's chest and rump to help her stand. "Todd. Priority one is to get some IV fluids in her."

Todd took the lightweight dog and cradled her against his chest. "You want me to try a half cup of food with her? See if she can keep it down?"

Hazel nodded. "No more than that. I'm guessing she'll eat anything we put in front of her. But she won't be able to digest much."

Interesting that Mr. Hanson, who claimed to be so attached to the dog his wife had allegedly taken from him and abused, didn't pet Athena or even try to talk to her as Todd carried her from the room. Nothing suspicious about that. Right.

"How long have you had Athena?" Hazel asked, once the door closed behind Todd.

"I told you. Just a few days. Margery took her."

Hazel pulled her reading glasses from the collar of her T-shirt and picked up her clipboard to make a notation on the dog's chart. "How long did you have her before that? Did you get her as a puppy? Rescue her? Take her in as a stray?"

"She kept showing up at work, lookin' for handouts." Even when he finally uncrossed his arms, Mr. Hanson's stance still looked defensive. "I'm on a road crew. We're paving a gravel road out in east Jackson County. I figured somebody dumped her out in the country."

Sadly, that might be true. Perhaps he thought he'd done a good thing by helping the dog find a home. But not if he didn't know how to, or couldn't, give the dog proper care. "Is she current on her shots? Has Athena had any vaccinations you know of?"

He pulled off his cap and scratched his thinning white hair. "I dunno."

Not the answer she was hoping for. "Don't take this the wrong way, Mr. Hanson, but...can you afford to keep a dog? There are programs through several vet clinics I work with that provide food and basic equipment like leashes and bedding, even medical care, for pets whose owners need a little extra help. Would you like me to put you in contact with them?"

Muttering something under his breath, he plunked the hat back on top of his head and started to pace. "What's with the twenty questions? Can you help her or not?"

Unless they found evidence of an internal parasite or illness, this was an easy diagnosis. And she hated it. "Right now, we'll treat Athena for starvation and dehydration." She removed her glasses and hugged the clipboard to her chest as she met the resentful glance he tossed her across the table. Probably every woman was on his hit list now. She'd proceed cautiously, but this dog wasn't going back to Hanson or his wife, not until animal control had investigated the case and she knew exactly who was responsible for the dog's deplorable condition. "I'd like to keep Athena here for at least forty-eight hours, to keep her under observation and make sure she's getting the care she needs. When she's stronger, we'll get a complete blood count, urinalysis and biochemistry profile to find out if there are any underlying issues causing her malnourishment. I'll call you with my results, of course."

"You're taking my dog, aren't you?" he muttered, sliding his chaw into the opposite cheek. The subtle movement struck Hazel as a pressure valve the man used to contain his temper. "You're gonna get me in trouble with the law." He circled around the table to trail his dirty fingers across the counter, touching the handle of every drawer and cabinet along the way. "I told you, it was Margery who let her get like that."

Hazel turned to keep him in her sight as he moved

behind her. "I don't have the authority to take your dog, Mr. Hanson. But if I can't find any evidence of a medical reason for her weight loss, then I will report your ex-wife for animal cruelty." She'd be putting his name on that report, too, as the registered owner.

"Do that." He stopped at the door to the lobby and squeezed the knob. "She took everything I had left. And that wasn't much. I'm just glad to get Athena back."

"Divorces can be hard. Even under the best of circumstances."

"Under the worst of circumstances, they're…" He faced her again, nodding toward the fingers she'd curled around her clipboard. "I see you ain't got no ring on your hand. You divorced, Dr. Cooper?"

Hazel curled her toes into her clogs, resisting the urge to back away from those icy gray eyes. "I am."

He splayed one hand on the metal table and the other on the countertop. He pressed a button on her computer keyboard, clearing the screen saver, before pushing down on the scale she used to weigh puppies, kittens and other small animals. The cradle bounced up and down as he released it. She respected a hardworking man and understood the grime that came with a construction job like his. But since this was a medical facility, there was a sterility factor she had to protect. When he reached toward the sharps disposal bin on the wall, she grabbed his wrist and stopped him. "Mr. Hanson, that's a potential biohazard. Some of this is expensive equipment, too. I ask you not to touch it."

"Yes, ma'am." She couldn't tell if that glimpse of yellowed teeth was a smile or a snarl. But he pulled away and crossed his arms over his gut again in that challenging stance he'd used earlier. "You have a successful business here, Dr. Cooper. Your ex pay for it?"

Hazel bristled at the question. "Excuse me?"

"Did you use his alimony to start your clinic?"

Alimony? That was a joke. When her marriage to Aaron had ended, there'd been nothing left to ask for. The simple answer was no, she'd started this clinic and paid off her student loans on her own dime. She didn't need anyone's help to be a good veterinarian and smart businesswoman. But Wade Hanson was practically a stranger. This was the first time she'd seen Athena as a patient. The dog was already three or four years old and hadn't been fixed or had her teeth cleaned. Other than this brief time they'd spent together in the exam room, she didn't know this man. He didn't need to know her history. "I'm here to take care of Athena—not tell you my life story." Since he wouldn't take the initiative to leave, she moved past him and opened the door for him. "I'll make sure she's eating and does her business before I send her home. Now, if you'll excuse me, I have another appointment."

"You never answered my question about starting this clinic."

"I don't intend to." Whatever prejudice he had against his ex-wife or divorced women, Hazel wasn't going to let him get away with the veiled insults.

"You'll notice that it's *my* name over the door, Mr. Hanson."

He grunted a smug sound that seemed to indicate he hadn't really expected her to share the details of her divorce, or that he didn't believe she had become a success in her own right. If Wade Hanson wanted sympathy or someone to commiserate with over the bitterness he felt for his ex-wife, he'd have to make an appointment with a therapist.

"I get the message, Dr. Cooper." He stepped through the open door, turning back to her, and said, "But you get this message. I intend to keep my dog. No woman is going to take him away from me again. I'll call or stop by tomorrow to see how she's doing."

The inner door opened behind her, and Hazel didn't think she'd ever been so happy to see Todd walk into a room. The interruption finally got Hanson moving.

"You're welcome to do that," she answered, dredging up a smile she didn't feel before closing the door after Wade Hanson. Her shoulders sagged in a weary sigh before she straightened again to face Todd. "Did you get Athena situated?"

"She's handling the IV just fine," he reported. "And she wolfed down that pâté like it was going out of style." He opened the door a crack and peeked out into the lobby before closing it again. "Did you get a load of that guy? He was more interested in getting the dog away from his wife than in taking care of it himself. You gonna report him to animal control?"

She'd like to report him for animal cruelty, female

bashing, failure to bathe and creeping her out for no good reason.

Instead, she simply nodded, putting on her reading glasses again and pulling up Athena's patient file on the computer to transfer her notations from the clipboard. "Whether it was Wade Hanson or his wife who let the dog get into this condition, it doesn't matter. Someone needs to be held responsible."

"Hey. You okay?" If Todd had put a hand on her, she probably would have snapped. But maybe he was finally learning the rules of conduct she expected from him. "You look a little rattled. You worried Hanson is going to retaliate if he loses his dog?"

She was worried about a lot of things lately. But she wasn't about to open up to her vet tech and give him any kind of encouragement to take their working relationship to a more personal level. "It's been a long day. I'm fine. Thanks for asking."

Todd's eyebrows came together atop his glasses in a frown. But when she refused to elaborate, he opened a cabinet door and pulled down a bottle of disinfectant spray and paper towels. "You want me to clean up in here? I'm happy to help."

"No, I'll do it. I need to get these details into the system before I call the authorities." Plus, she needed to listen to the messages on her phone. If they were all from Aaron, she'd report them to his parole officer, Steve Kranitz. She continued typing. "Tell the front desk I'm taking a short break. I'll be right out."

"You got it." He exited into the main lobby, closing the door behind him.

Alone in the quiet for the first time that day, Hazel rolled out the stool from beneath the counter and sank onto it. She puffed out a weary breath that lifted her bangs off her forehead before she saved the information on the screen and pulled her phone from her jeans.

"Damn it." Six missed calls, all from Aaron.

And one more from a number she didn't recognize that had just come through. She tried to feel hopeful that at least it wasn't the number of the man who had called and threatened her last night. But Burke had said it was easy to buy several burner phones to prevent KCPD from tracing the calls.

Maybe it was a wrong number.

And maybe her stalker got off on finding one insidious way after another to contact her. To declare his love or frighten her or threaten her with whatever his sick agenda might be.

After pulling up her voice mail, she set the phone on the countertop. Before playing her messages, she ripped off a handful of paper towels and picked up the disinfectant spray, keeping her hands busy and pretending to divert her thoughts by cleaning as she listened.

The polite request in Aaron's first two messages turned to frustration and blew up into a curse-filled tirade by the last one. *"Don't make me fill up your voice mail with messages. Pick up the damn phone and talk to me. Or tell me where and when we can meet. We have to talk. I heard what happened to Polly's car. What if she'd been in it, Hazel? Clearly, you can't handle what's happening on your own. Screw your independence. You need me. The girls need me. I'm their father and I'm worried."* Several beats of silence passed, and Hazel stopped wiping down the scale cradle, thinking the message had ended. But just when she moved to save it as evidence for Officer Kranitz, Aaron exhaled a noisy breath and spoke in a calmer tone. *"I blamed you for putting me in prison. But this one could be on me. I may have some enemies. Let me help."*

The message ended with another recitation of his cell number and a beep. Hazel saved the message and returned with an almost compulsive need to wipe down every knob and surface Wade Hanson had touched. If only she could wipe away the memories of every man who was unhappy with her lately—every man who might be responsible for this psychological torture of love letters and threats and bombs.

I may have some enemies.

"You think?" Try over three hundred enemies who'd lost their life savings and retirement funds to her greedy ex. Or the man he'd pointed a finger at as an accomplice during his trial in an effort to get his sentence reduced. Hazel's testimony had put them both behind bars. And that list of potential enemies didn't account for anyone Aaron might have butted heads with during his fifteen-year stint in prison.

The last message started to play, cooling Hazel's manic energy. She stopped working and stared at the phone on the counter, as if it was responsible for the sudden chill in the air around her.

She heard breathing that was measured and crackling with a slight wheeze. When her caller spoke, the voice sounded eerily familiar. *"Ten...nine...eight... Do you feel the clock ticking yet?"* Could Aaron have disguised his voice to the point she didn't recognize it? Had he coerced a friend into calling on his behalf? Or was there some other obsessive lunatic in her life she hadn't yet identified? *"My patience with you is running out, my beloved. Give me what I want. Or I'll take it from you."*

"Take what!" She slammed the bottle down on the counter. "What the hell do you want from me?"

A soft knock on the door reminded her that she'd raised her voice. Was there a client in the lobby, or had someone from her staff overheard her?

She punched off her cell and stashed it in her pocket as Ashley nudged her way inside the exam room. Her green eyes were narrowed with concern as she closed the door behind her. "Mom? You okay?"

"Hi, sweetie." Hazel tossed the soiled towels and put away the disinfectant, buying herself a few seconds to regain her composure before she pointed to the clipboard her daughter carried. "That my next patient?"

"Your last appointment for the day. It's a new patient." Ashley hugged the clipboard to the front of her pink scrubs. "Who was that on the phone?"

"I was listening to my messages." Hazel reached for the printout of patient information.

Instead of handing it over, Ashley tucked the clipboard behind her back. "Who left the messages? I can't tell if that's your worried face or your pissed-off face. But neither is good. I was hoping you'd be in a better mood, because I need to ask you a favor."

"What favor?"

Ashley pointed to Hazel's head. "Explain the face first."

She'd go with the lesser of two evils. Or maybe she was a fool to think either caller was less of a threat than the other. "Have you gotten any phone calls from your father?"

"From Dad? Dad called you?" Ashley shook her head. "No. Not since he first got out of prison and he begged to meet with Polly and me behind your back. That's when the judge expanded that restraining order to include us." Moving closer, she leaned her hip against the counter. "I'm not sure I'd even recognize what he sounds like anymore, unless he identified himself. What did he say?"

What was the best way to explain this honestly, without tainting her daughter's perception of her father? "He saw the news story about Polly's car and the bomb threat here. He wants to make sure you're both okay."

"He cares now? He didn't care sixteen years ago when all those people were so angry with him and our family."

"He's older. He's had a lot of time to think on what he did and what he lost." Hazel shoved her hands into the pockets of her jacket and shrugged. "He claims that prison has changed him."

"Yeah, but how? What if it just made him a smarter

criminal who can't be caught now? Or do you think he really cares?"

"I can't answer that. I know he adored you both when you were little." Hazel leaned against the counter, giving Ashley's shoulder a teasing bump with her own. "I always promised that when you and Polly were of age, if you wanted a relationship with your father, I wouldn't stand in your way."

"Yeah, well, he used to love you, too." Ashley shook her head, dismissing any idea of reconciliation. "Mom, we know what he did to you. Even now that I'm old enough to understand his supposed reasons, I can't forgive him for that. He didn't know how to be a good father then, and I doubt that's a skill one learns in prison."

"So you don't want to have contact with him?" Hazel reached over to pull Ashley's ponytail from the collar of her top and smoothed it down her back. "Don't answer right away. Think about it."

"I don't need to think about it. Polly and I have discussed it more than once. We don't really know him. We don't want to. We don't want him to be a part of our lives."

"I'll talk to him, then. Or rather, I'll have my attorney talk to his." With her mood lifted, Hazel pushed away from the counter. "Now, what about this favor?"

Ashley's expression creased with a smile she could barely contain. "Well, maybe I can help your day end on a more positive note."

The smile was contagious. "I'm all for that."

"Do you need me to stay for this last appointment?

Joe's coming here to take me to dinner. I'd like to change before he picks me up."

"Joe's coming here?"

"Yes. I thought you might like to check him out for yourself and see how sweet he is. After everything that happened yesterday, I thought that might ease your mind a little bit."

Hazel nodded, appreciating the thoughtful plan. "I think it might."

"Great." She handed Hazel the clipboard she'd brought in. "Here's the chart for Mr. Jingles. Looks like a standard checkup for a newly adopted pet."

Hazel scanned the printout on her new feline patient. "I think I can handle one cat without help." Ashley was already heading out the door to the lobby when Hazel stopped her. "Wait. What about Polly? Will she be on her own tonight?"

"I already talked to Sergeant Burke. He's picking her up at the hospital and taking her home. Polly's cool with that. She has to study for a test tomorrow, so she won't be going anywhere." Ashley gave her a quick hug, then practically danced out the door. "Thanks. I'll let you know as soon as Joe gets here."

"Wait. Ash?" She followed her daughter into the lobby. "When did you talk to Sergeant—"

"Excuse me? I'm Mr. Jingles's owner." A hand with polished French-tip nails was suddenly thrust toward her, stopping Hazel in her tracks.

She instinctively took the woman's hand. "Hello."

"Thank you for working me into your busy sched-

ule, Dr. Cooper." The dark-haired woman wore a polished gray suit and held a carrier with a cat that was
equally sleek and dark. "I'm Shannon Bennett."

Chapter Eight

Burke checked his watch and swore. He tapped on the accelerator, pushing his speed as much as he could without turning on his siren.

He was the only one with an emergency here. If he didn't feel it like a fist to the gut every time Hazel's eyes darkened with fear or uncertainty, he wouldn't care so much about running late now that he and Gunny were off the clock. But it was nearly 5:30 p.m. And though he knew she would be the last one to leave her clinic after locking up, he'd gotten caught up in a search on the grounds at the KCI Airport that had required a team effort by KCPD and airport security to cover a large search grid after a multiple-bomb threat had been called in and a suspicious bag had been discovered in a culvert off one of the parking lots. Fortunately, the bag had ended up being an extreme case of lost luggage, and the depressed individual who'd called in the threat had been identified sitting in his car in another parking lot. He'd been apprehended and taken to a hospital. But now Burke's clothes and skin were damp with the rain, his boots were muddy and he smelled like wet dog.

But he'd promised Hazel he'd be there to protect her and her family. Knowing her independent streak, she'd walk across the parking lot and drive home alone, just as she had all those years when there'd been no one in her life to look out for her. She was a smart woman, and strong. But a stalker who knew so much about her, and so much about explosives, created dangerous circumstances that required her to be extra careful regarding her security. Hell, had he reminded her of the basic safety precautions of checking under and around her truck before even approaching it? Did she understand situational awareness? Pinpointing the location of every person in her vicinity, taking note of her surroundings and anything that seemed out of place?

Would she call him if something *did* seem out of place?

He peered through the rhythmic sweep of the windshield wipers to race through a yellow light and cross into the industrial area north of downtown where her veterinary clinic and a neighboring dog park were located. Even though he and Gunny had put in a long day, he wanted to have his partner do a sweep of Hazel's truck before she got in, just in case the perp who was terrorizing her made good on last night's threat and had escalated from blowing up her daughter's unoccupied car into a much more personal attack.

Burke eyed his cell phone in the console beside

him, wondering if he should try calling her again. But since his first two messages about waiting for him had gone straight to voice mail, he focused on weaving through rush hour traffic and getting to the clinic as quickly as he could. Either she was busy, ignoring him or he was already way too late. And that was what made everything in him tighten with worry.

His blood pressure dropped a fraction when he spotted the familiar sign of her family animal clinic. He flipped on his turn signal and slowed but had to stomp on the brake as he came up behind a gray sedan that was nearly the same color as the rain. The pricey car was parked at the curb just outside the clinic parking lot. Not the safest place to park, so close to the driveway entrance. The dark-haired driver was going to get her fancy bumper clipped if she wasn't careful.

Taking a wide arc around the sedan, Burke entered the nearly empty parking lot. Relieved to see Hazel's truck, he pulled in a parking stall and shrugged into his still-wet KCPD jacket before he heard the squeal of tires against the wet payment. Climbing out, he adjusted the bill of his cap to protect his eyes from the rain and saw the taillights of the gray sedan speeding away. Maybe the police logo on the side of his truck had made the driver think twice about creating a potential traffic hazard. Or else the driver had been parked there for no good reason.

Wait a minute.

"No way." He pulled Gunny from the truck and jogged to the street. But the gray sedan had merged with traffic and disappeared. Dark-haired woman in a fancy car? She'd been wearing sunglasses, despite the gloomy weather. He hadn't seen her face, and he no longer knew what his ex-wife drove, but that couldn't have been Shannon, could it?

How could she have known he was coming here? Had she asked one of the men on his team? He was off the clock, so even Dispatch didn't know his twenty. Was she so desperate to reconnect with him that she'd hoped for a face-to-face meeting?

His hand hovered over the phone in his vest beneath his jacket while the rain drummed against the bill of his cap. No. He wouldn't give his ex the satisfaction of calling her to ask where she was, and he dropped his hand to Gunny's flank.

Maybe it hadn't been Shannon in that car at all. She'd been on his mind as an annoyance he needed to deal with ever since last night's call. He needed to sit down with her and spell out that they were never going to get back together. His heart belonged to someone else now. He'd just projected Shannon's identity onto the random brunette the way a supposed eyewitness would sometimes misidentify a suspect because their concentration had been off-line due to their emotions.

Unless… Burke planed the water off his cheeks and jaw and turned back toward the clinic door. Could Shannon have been spying on Hazel? Checking out her competition? Not that there was any possibility of a reunion, but it might be worth looking up the make of her car and, if it was a match, paying her a visit. There were already enough things standing in the way of the relationship he wanted with Hazel. The threats. Preserving a friendship. Hazel's stubborn self-protection streak. He didn't need a jealous ex thrown into the mix working against the future he envisioned for them, too.

With an urgent *"Voran,"* he guided Gunny over to Hazel's truck and ordered the dog to search.

He was stowing Gunny in the back seat of his truck after a quick towel off and a dog biscuit when the clinic doors opened. Hazel stepped out and put up a blue umbrella against the steady drone of the rain.

She scooped Cleo into her arms and handed the small dog over to the young couple who followed her out and waited beside her while she locked the door. He recognized Ashley's long blond ponytail as the two women hugged. The young dark-haired man with a tattoo snaking up his neck and a bandanna tied around the top of his head was someone new, and Burke shifted inside his boots, forcing himself to stay put, trying not to make a suspect of every man who got close to Hazel. The young man and Ashley were both wearing bulky rain pants and jackets. Burke had already spotted the motorcycle parked across the lot from his truck and suspected that Tattoo Man belonged to the bike.

Hazel shook hands with the younger man, turning as Ashley beamed a smile at Burke and waved. "Hey, Burke!"

Burke touched the brim of his cap at her enthusiastic greeting. "Hey, Ash."

In a swift move known only to escape artists and matchmaking daughters, Ashley handed the dog back to her mother, slipped behind her and nudged Hazel forward, pulling the man with her in the opposite direction. Burke shook his head at the totally unsubtle move. At least he had one Cooper woman who was in favor of him getting together with Hazel. Ashley and the guy who was apparently her date hurried down the steps to the left of the door, where they unpacked their helmets from the storage compartment on his motorcycle.

Hazel walked down the ramp in the opposite direction at a much slower pace, meeting Burke at her truck, depositing Cleo and her purse inside before facing him. She raised her umbrella over Burke's head so that it sheltered both. "Here you are, showing up at my clinic again. Is this going to be a thing now?"

"Me keeping you safe? I think so."

She eyed his sodden, muddy appearance from hat to toe before narrowing her eyes as she frowned. "Is there a problem?"

"Long day. Turned out okay."

"But I saw you and Gunny searching my truck."

"Overdeveloped protective instincts," he joked. "Just your friendly neighborhood cop making sure you and Cleo get safely home." He thumbed over his shoulder at his truck and the weary working dog relaxing inside. "Gunny didn't hit on any explosives. I wouldn't have let you and the one-eyed fuzz ball anywhere near your truck if he had."

Finally, she smiled, a regular ol' friendly smile,

as though she was glad to see him, and not over-thinking or regretting the changing status of their relationship. "Cleo and I thank you. Are you coming over for dinner?"

"Would I be welcome?"

"Me spending time with you? I think so." She gave his teasing right back, and his pulse kicked up a notch at the idea of kissing that beautiful smile.

Fortunately, he had wet clothes cooling on his skin and work that still needed to be done to temper his instinctive male reaction to sharing the intimate space beneath the umbrella with her while the rain falling around them cocooned them from the rest of the world. "I won't be there right away. After I drive Polly to her apartment, I've got a couple of leads on your case I want to follow up on."

"Leads? Like what?"

Besides checking with Justin Grant and the crime lab on the details surrounding the bomb parts mailed to Hazel, and those used to blow up Polly's car, Burke thought of the dark-haired woman in the car who had sped away. "Who was that woman who just drove off?"

Hazel glanced around the parking lot. "What woman?"

"The brunette in the BMW."

"My last client left half an hour ago. A routine check on her new cat, Mr. Jingles. She was chatty. He was fine." She nodded toward the couple climbing onto the motorcycle. "Ashley and Joe and I are the only ones here."

"Your last client wasn't Shannon Bennett, was it?"

"Yes. How did you…?" She leaned away from him, scanning the parking lot again. "Wait. *Your* Shannon? The last name was different. I've never met her before… I was focused on the cat, and I didn't think… Was she checking me out? Does she think something's going on between us?"

Hell, yeah, there was something going on between them. Exactly what hadn't been determined yet, but he wouldn't deny the connection between them anymore. "It doesn't matter what she thinks. Shannon's no longer a part of my life, and I don't want her to be a part of yours."

"She was waiting here until you came. To see if you were going to show up." Hazel shoved her bangs off her forehead. They were damp enough to stick up in a wild disarray. "Is she one of those leads you're following up on? You think a woman could be responsible for what's happening to me?"

Burke wasn't ruling out anyone who might be a threat to Hazel. But his ex-wife was at the bottom of his list of suspects. "Shannon has zero access to explosives, and she wouldn't know how to put a bomb together."

"She could have hired someone who does." Frustration was evident as she attacked her sticky bangs again. "If she blames me for stealing you from her—"

"I've been making my own decisions about who I want to be with for a long time now. There is no stealing. I choose."

"And you choose me."

"Damn right, I do."

"But if she's jealous, we should…"

Hazel's smile had faded. Burke wanted it back. "Forget about Shannon. Our marriage was over years ago. I'll have a conversation with her. She won't bother you again." He wasn't giving Hazel another excuse to push aside the feelings that had finally surfaced between them. "Drive straight home to the parking garage." He pulled his keys from his pocket and stepped from beneath the umbrella. "I'll meet you at your place when I'm finished. And I'll bring dinner."

"You don't have to do that."

He strode to his truck. "I'll be there in an hour. Hour and a half, tops."

Hazel grabbed his arm to stop him, sliding the umbrella over his head again. "Jedediah—"

"Gunny's worried about Cleo. He'd like to make sure she's safe and fed and locked in for the night."

She arched a silvery-gold eyebrow. "Gunny's worried?"

This silly conversation was safer than pouring his guts out to her again the way he had last night. "If Gunny had a driver's license, he'd come over by himself. But he needs me to be his chauffeur."

"Oh, well, tell him we're in the mood for something light tonight, like a salad. It's the only way Cleo and I can justify the ice-cream sundae we intend to eat for dessert."

"With your homemade caramel sauce?" He thought of her licking that spoon again and wondered why, since a few decades had passed since he'd been a horny teenager, his body reacted so sharply, so instantly, to the thought of her licking things. Like him. *Wow.* He needed to feel the cool rain splashing in his face again. Since he'd given in to that kiss, his body seemed to have a one-track mind where Dr. Hazel Cooper was concerned. "Is there enough to share?"

"I'll make sure there is." She glanced back to her truck. "Cleo is looking forward to seeing Gunny again this evening."

"Gunny's pretty stoked about it, too."

They weren't fooling anybody here, least of all each other. Hazel reached up and brushed away the moisture pooling on his shoulders. Her fingers hooked beneath the front of his jacket to straighten his collar and settled there. All casual touches. Every one adding to the energy that hummed through him when they were close like this.

"All this innuendo is dangerous for my peace of mind," she confessed. It was reassuring to hear that, although she was fighting the chemistry they shared, she wasn't denying it. "It makes me feel like you and I are becoming *us*."

He feathered his fingers into her hair and smoothed her bangs back into place across the smooth, warm skin of her forehead. "We are, Haze. I believe in *us*. One day, you will, too. As long as we're on the journey together, I'll go as slow as you need me to."

Hazel shook her head. "That's hardly fair to you."

He cupped his hand against her cheek and jaw. "You're worth the wait."

She studied him for several silent seconds, gauging his sincerity before turning her lips into the palm of his hand and pressing a kiss there. "I want to know anything you find out."

"Will do."

Her fingers flexed inside the front of his jacket, as though she'd forgotten she was still holding on to him. He hadn't. "And thank you for taking care of Polly this evening. You score a lot of brownie points with that."

He liked brownie points. He liked the idea of redeeming them with her even better. "You raised two good people. I'm happy to help them where I can."

The motorcycle engine roared to life, diverting their attention to the opposite side of the parking lot. With the tats, the muscles and the Harley, Ashley's date looked tough. But that alone didn't make him a threat. The young man made sure Ashley had her helmet securely fastened, and he'd waited for the two women to lock up the clinic earlier. Ashley didn't seem to have any problem winding her arms around his waist as he turned his bike toward the street.

"Bye, Mom! Burke!" Ashley waved before latching onto him again and leaning into his back as he revved the motor and pulled out of the lot.

"Have fun," Hazel called after her, but they were already racing away down the street.

Burke watched Hazel wrap both hands around the base of her umbrella. Any tighter and the wood might snap. "Is that the boyfriend?"

"'Fraid so. Joe Sciarra. He's a bouncer she met at

a bar." Her grip didn't relax until the couple had disappeared into the camouflage of traffic and rain. "He was actually charming and well-spoken," she admitted, "although he looks like he rides with one of those motorcycle gangs."

"Want me to run a background check on him?"

Green eyes swiveled up to his. "Can you do that? Isn't that an abuse of your position on the force?"

"Yes, and yes."

"I don't want to get you into trouble."

"One of the perks of running my own division is that I've earned enough clout to call in favors if I need to. The department will give me a little leeway if I ask for it." Since he had no idea yet who was targeting Hazel, this was a no-brainer. "There have been enough threats that I can justify getting the background on anyone suspicious in your circle of friends and acquaintances."

She considered his answer for a moment, then nodded. "Then, while you're at it, could you also run a background check on a Wade Hanson?"

"Who's that?"

"A client of mine. He's got a pretty serious grudge against women. Still, I just met him today, so he couldn't have sent all those letters."

A bad feeling twisted inside him. "Did he threaten you?"

"Not directly."

"Damn it, Haze—I told you to call—"

She splayed her fingers against his chest, quieting him with a gentle touch. "You can't stop me from doing my job. Just like I can't stop you from doing yours. I suspect him either of animal abuse or failing to report the abuse. I had to call animal control on him, and I doubt that will make him happy with me."

Burke covered her hand with his, needing the anchor of her calm strength to keep from going into protective-caveman mode and scaring her away from confiding in him. "Wade Hanson. Got it. Anything else you want to tell me?" he teased, trying to lighten his mood. He didn't expect to see the frown tighten her expression. Ah, hell. There *was* something else. "What is it?"

"Later. There are some messages on my phone I want you to listen to." Hazel fisted her fingers into the front of his jacket and stretched onto her toes to press a sweet kiss to the corner of his mouth. He treasured the gift without trying to turn it into anything more. "Go do what you need to do. Find answers for me. And tell Gunny not to be late."

HAZEL SUSPECTED THE low-lying areas of the city would be flooding by now with all this rain. But the intermittent downpours kept her neighbors from asking any questions as she walked Cleo inside the perimeter of the parking garage. The other residents of the building exchanged a friendly greeting or stopped to pet Cleo when they came home from work or errands. While she appreciated the security of knowing concrete and steel grating surrounded the ground level of her building, keeping threats and unwanted visitors out of her life, she didn't want them asking why she wasn't walking her dog across the street in the minipark or up a couple of blocks on the grassy area between her neighborhood and the wall that blocked the highway at the base of the hill.

Because someone keeps threatening to blow me up.

Nope, she didn't want to have to explain that one—or try to come up with a lie that would convince them that they were safe, even though she lived in the building with them.

One advantage to having a three-legged dog was that she didn't have to walk Cleo very far to get her exercise. A couple of laps around the garage was enough for Cleo to do both her businesses and clean up after her.

One *dis*advantage to having a three-legged dog was that she didn't have to walk Cleo very far to get her exercise. Security aside, Hazel felt entombed behind the garage's metal gate. Mist from the rain filtered through the steel mesh walls and made the air feel heavy. It trapped the scents of oil and dog, and the sharp, earthy smells of waterlogged foliage and mud from the landscaping outside. Although she knew it would be foolish to do so, she longed to get out into the evening air and feel the rain cool her skin and see it wash the sidewalks clean. She could feel the wind if she was out in the open, and maybe that would blow away this sense of uneasiness that left her starting at every new sound and counting the minutes until Burke showed up with dinner and that heavenly smell that was all man and uniquely his.

She needed to figure out what she was feeling and

decide where she wanted her future with Burke to go. He'd been too good a friend for too long for her to give him false hope. She wouldn't be selfish and string him along just so she wouldn't lose his caring and companionship. She was a mature woman who hadn't known passion for a long time, but every fiber of her body craved his kisses and the firm, needy touches that had awakened her long-dormant desire. And no woman of any age would want to deny herself the tenderness and respect with which he treated her.

Hazel cared about Burke. She enjoyed spending time with him—eating, working, talking. They shared a devotion to animals and justice and protecting the people they cared about. She admitted a healthy lust for his toned body and grizzled jaw and teasing sense of humor.

But did she love him? Could she surrender her whole heart to him?

Because if she changed her life—if she let herself love again—she wasn't doing anything halfway. Jedediah Burke wasn't a halfway kind of man, either. And that meant it wouldn't halfway hurt if she made the wrong choice.

Although the rational part of her brain insisted on arguing the point, Hazel was beginning to think that, deep inside, she'd already made her decision. The fact that she didn't want to go back upstairs to her lonely place by herself, now that Burke and Gunny had filled up her condo with their presence, was very telling. Maybe Ashley and Polly—and Burke—were right. The only person standing in the way of a second chance at happiness was her.

And the nimrod who kept taunting her with the promise of blowing her to smithereens.

"That's one hell of a pep talk, Dr. Coop," she muttered out loud. "Cleo, what do you think I should do?"

The dog tilted her head up at the mention of her name, and Hazel reached down to scratch around the schnauzer's ears. But the need for affection lasted only a few seconds before Cleo put her nose to the ground and followed an intriguing scent around a parked car to the concrete half wall.

"Good advice," Hazel praised. "Keep yourself busy instead of worrying so much."

Hazel decided that instead of checking her watch every few minutes like a schoolgirl waiting for her first date to pick her up, she'd find something to keep herself busy and out of her head. She pulled her phone from the pocket of her jeans and called Polly.

"Hey, Mom," her younger daughter answered, clearly recognizing her number on the screen of her phone. "Checking up on me?" she teased in a breathy voice. "Or checking up on Sergeant Burke? He left here about an hour ago. Said he was stopping by the precinct office to do some research. He asked if you like taco salad. I said yes."

"He's coming over for dinner tonight to check on me."

"I kind of figured."

Based on the rhythmic cadence of Polly's voice,

Hazel guessed her daughter was in the middle of a workout. "You're not out running tonight, are you?"

"No, worrywart," Polly chided with affection. "Yoga. I'm playing one of those exercise DVDs. I won't get soaked in the rain and catch a cold, and no bad guys can chase me."

Hazel followed Cleo along the wall as the small schnauzer tracked the path of whatever had piqued her interest. "Will you be all right by yourself? Do you want to come over here until Ashley gets home?"

"And be a third wheel on your date with Burke? No, thanks."

"It's not a date."

"It should be."

Hazel heaved a deep sigh that echoed Polly's tension-clearing breath. "I need to work through some things before I commit to a new relationship."

"Mom." Her daughter dragged the single word out to three syllables on three different pitches. "You've had sixteen years to work through things after Dad. You have the right to be happy. If you don't grab Burke, someone else will."

As they reached the wide mesh gate at the parking garage entrance, Cleo jerked on her leash, pulling Hazel down the ramp toward the sidewalk, insisting on tracking the scent outside. *What in the world?* Had one of the neighborhood cats sauntered past? Hazel gave a short tug on the leash. "Come on, girl. You don't want to be out in the rain, and neither do I."

"Sounds like Cleo needs your attention. I swear, you spoil that dog more than you ever did Ash or me."

Hazel could hear the smile in her daughter's voice and remembered when she'd been that full of energy and certain that everything would turn out all right if she worked hard, stayed hopeful and remained loyal to the people she loved. That had been a lifetime ago, before Aaron's arrest and the divorce. Before the night she nearly died. Hazel planted her feet as Cleo jerked against the leash. When had she gotten so old and cynical? How long had surviving her life been more important than living it? Too long. She'd taught her daughters better but had reached fifty and was no longer practicing what she preached. "Mom? You still there?"

"Yes. Sorry, I got distracted." Hazel vowed to change her life. Right now. She wasn't going to be a coward about living anymore. And if grabbing Jedediah Burke was part of that spiritual renaissance, then so be it. "You're an insightful young woman, Polly Cooper."

"Um, thanks?"

"I have to go." Her gaze followed the length of the leash down to Cleo to see what had caught the dog's attention. Hazel spotted the vague outline of something small but oddly shaped leaning against the garage gate. But the lights from inside the garage cast distorting shadows through the steel mesh, and she couldn't quite make it out. Were those little tufts of fur poking through the bottom links of the gate? Had a small animal taken refuge from the rain? "I think I've made a decision."

"Good. Talking on the phone is messing with my

concentration." Polly laughed before taking another deep breath. "Call if you need anything. Good luck with Burke. Love you."

"Love you, too. Bye." Cleo was pawing at one of the tufts of fur, pulling it through the gate. Was that…a tail? "Cleo. Stop." Hazel knelt and ran her hand along the dog's back to calm the frantic thrill of discovery. "What have you found, girl?"

Whatever belonged to that striped tail wasn't moving. Shortening Cleo's leash, she tucked it beneath the sole of her boot to keep the dog away from the creature that could be ill or worse. She turned on the flashlight on her phone and shone the light through the gate. She gasped a quick inhale of compassion.

A cat.

"Oh, sweetie, what's happened to you?" The veterinarian in her quickly squelched her sympathy and she pushed to her feet. A stray must have curled up as close to shelter as it could get and breathed its last breath. Or else some coldhearted clown who shouldn't be responsible for an animal had lost a pet and dumped the creature here instead of paying for a cremation or disposing of it legally.

Hazel hurried to the pedestrian door. She would check the cat's condition for herself and make sure there was no contagious illness or even take it back to the clinic to scan for a microchip. She'd already called animal control once today. She wasn't afraid to make the owner accountable if there was one.

But Hazel froze before pushing open the locked door. Besides the cat at the vehicle entrance, there was something leaning against the bottom of the door here, too. This object had clean, straight lines instead of curves. It was covered in brown paper instead of fur.

Her vision spun with trepidation as she squatted down to inspect the oblong package that had been left just outside her secure sanctuary. She didn't need to see her name on the mailing label to know what it was, to know it was for her.

But she read it, anyway. *Hazel Cooper.* With her home address.

She shivered as the damp air penetrated her skin. She scooped Cleo up into her arms and made herself breathe, so she wouldn't pass out with fear. Or anger.

Not again. Not here.

Hazel snapped a picture of the package with her phone, then texted it to Burke's number.

He's been here. Left a package. Calling 911.

A shadow fell over Hazel, and Cleo twisted in her arms, barking as though they were under attack.

Hazel looked up at the furious noise.

And screamed.

Chapter Nine

The grotesque features of the red-and-black Halloween mask framed by the hood of the man's jacket
quickly took shape. But identifying the devil cos-
tume made him no less frightening than the monster
that had first startled her. His eyes were recessed
behind the mask, shadowed by night and impossible
to identify.

Tumbling onto her butt in her haste to retreat,
Hazel scrambled away, clutching the growling, barking Cleo to her chest. Even though the steel grating
and coded locks kept him from reaching her, it didn't
stop the man from curling one set of his black-gloved
fingers through the steel links.

And breathing.

He didn't say a single word, but she could hear
his breath coming in gusts and gasps, as though he
was out of shape or had run up on her fast. Had he
hoped she'd step outside to check on the cat? Maybe
trip the bomb when she opened the door? Grab her
as soon as she was on his side of the security gate?

Or maybe this sicko was simply excited to see how badly he'd startled her.

She quickly got to her feet, hugging Cleo as tightly as the squirming, snarling dog allowed. "Get away from me!" she warned.

The only thing that moved was his chest, puffing in and out as he did that damn breathing. The man's dark jeans and hoodie were soaked with rain and dripping onto the sidewalk. He'd probably been standing outside for a while, no doubt watching her, and she hadn't even realized it. He'd been watching, waiting for her to be alone, waiting for her to move exactly where he wanted her before he approached. He was a dark, shapeless bulk without a human face, oozing malice and a power she didn't want him to have over her. The bottom of his mask puckered as he sucked in a deep breath, and for a moment, she thought he was going to speak. Instead, he reached into his pocket and pulled out an envelope. The dark holes of his eyes never wavered from her as he rolled the envelope into a scroll and pushed it through the grate.

Hazel watched the curled paper drop to the damp concrete in front of her.

"I'm not going to read that." It was hard to tear her gaze away from the sightless holes where his eyes should be. "Keep your damn love letters." She glanced one way toward the package, the other toward the feline corpse. "Stop bringing me these sick gifts. You need to leave me and my family alone. You're making me angry. Not afraid."

He stepped closer and she jumped back a step,

making a liar of herself. Okay, so she was angry *and* afraid. But she wasn't helpless, not entirely.

It took several seconds to hear her own thoughts through the muffling drumbeat of rain, Cleo's barking and her roiling emotions. *Do something. Put him on the defensive. Fight back.*

Suddenly, she felt the phone still clasped in her hand and raised it to snap a picture of the man. He flinched at the flash and spun away for a moment. "How do you like that? I'm calling the cops. I'm sending them a picture of you."

Hazel forwarded the image to Burke's phone, then snapped another picture. And another. Not bothering to read the answering texts from Burke.

The man came back, perhaps remembering that his disguise wouldn't give him away. That he had the advantages of strength and anonymity—and possibly a bomb—on his side of the metal links that separated them.

Her phone vibrated with another response, and she finally looked down at the flurry of texts from Burke.

On my way, said one text.

The next read, Go upstairs and lock yourself in. I notified Dispatch. Help is on its way.

Get the hell away from him! read the most recent message.

Hazel retreated another step. With no gun, he couldn't shoot her. With the gate between them, he couldn't reach her. And yet...

Her devilish suitor leaned into the grating, pushing it slightly forward with the weight of his body. He curled his gloved fingers through the links, stretching them toward her, making her feel as though he could touch her.

"Stay away from me." Hazel shook hard enough that Cleo halted her barking and nuzzled her mama's cheek. "It's okay, girl."

But it wasn't. If Hazel gave in to her imagination, the man would dematerialize and slide straight through the steel mesh to get to her.

"Give me what I want," he wheezed in a toneless whisper, finally deigning to speak.

Did she recognize that voice? It sounded like an echo of something familiar, but with its harsh rasp, she couldn't place it. Could she recognize him by his build? Smell? Anything? She hugged Cleo closer to her chest. "Who are you? What do you want from me?"

And then she saw the electronic device he held in his right hand, small enough to fit within his palm. He stroked it with his thumb. A tiny cell phone? A remote? Whatever it was, she didn't for one second believe it was anything good.

"What is that?" she demanded.

"On…" He flipped a cap off one end and pressed a button. Hazel swung her gaze over to the package, instinctively retreating. "Off…"

She flinched when he pushed the button again, expecting her world to erupt with flame and blow her into a gazillion pieces. She looked at him.

"There are innocent people in this building. You'd hurt more than you and me." She pleaded with him to remember his humanity. "Or don't you care how many people you hurt?"

His answer was an angry grunt. He charged the fence, sending a ripple of the rattling noise around the chain-link walls of the garage. "You should talk," he wheezed.

"Me? What did I do?" Hazel punched 9. "I've had enough of these games. I'm calling the police." Then 1. "Why don't you stay there and keep talking to me? Give them a chance to meet you, too." Another 1, and she hit the call button, then put the phone to her ear. "My name is Dr. Hazel Cooper. There's a man at my building. Threatening me. He has a package—I think it's a bomb. He already blew up my daughter's car." She rattled off her building address and the names of the detectives she'd been working with. "I've alerted my friend Sergeant Burke. Jedediah Burke. He runs the K-9 unit. He'll need backup." The man in the mask never moved, except to curl his black-gloved fingers into fists around the links. Not even hearing that police officers, the bomb squad and one very big, very bad K-9 cop who'd sworn to protect her were on their way could budge him.

"They'll be here any minute," Hazel warned him, repeating the dispatcher's last words. "KCPD is coming for you."

His response was to pull his fingers from the grate and slowly stroke the metal links as though he was caressing her face or her hair in some creepy pantomime of a gentle touch.

Hazel shivered. "Stop that."

The man caressed the metal one more time before turning the shadowed eye sockets of his mask toward the concrete floor and the envelope he'd delivered to her.

She shook her head, refusing to do as he asked. "What have I done that's worth killing me for? Worth killing yourself? If you set off that bomb now, you'll die, too. That's not much of a victory, is it?"

No answer.

"Did you kill that poor cat?"

He held up the device in his hand, pushed a button. "On," he whispered.

As much as she wanted him to go away, Hazel realized she needed to keep him here until the police arrived, instead of running for cover or tossing accusations that might scare him away. "All right. I'll read your note." She set Cleo down but kept the dog on a short leash—away from the man—as she stooped down to pick up the envelope and open it. There wasn't much to the typewritten letter inside.

You're going to be mine. Do you know how much I want from you? How much I need you to give me? Everything.

Everything?

Not *I want you*, but he wanted something *from* her.

Hazel raised her gaze to those missing eyes as understanding dawned. These weren't love letters. They were payback. The bombs and threats were about retribution this bastard thought she owed him.

For what? Something she had done? Some perceived slight? Could this terror campaign be payback for something Aaron had done in prison? Did this perv mistakenly think that hurting her would hurt her ex-husband?

Or was this Aaron himself? After so many years apart, would she recognize her own husband if he was disguised like this? Was this some twisted version of what Aaron had done to her all those years ago?

"Aaron?" She squinted through the glare of the garage lights and the shadows beyond them, trying to see his eyes behind the mask, searching for something familiar beneath the shapeless hoodie and baggy jeans. "Is that you? Why are you doing this?"

All he did was breathe.

Maybe this wasn't her ex. But then, Aaron hadn't actually done the dirty work the last time he'd terrorized her, either.

"Why?" There was no answer, of course. She lurched toward the grate, smacked it with the flat of her hand. Cleo barked at the sharp rattling noise. When the man jumped back from the figurative assault, it was very telling. *That* was a lot like Aaron, too. "Coward! Show me your face. Talk to me like a real man."

She hated the tears that stung her eyes. They were a toxic mix of remembered shock and fear, and anger that her life should come back to the nightmare that she'd barely survived sixteen years ago.

"Talk to me," she pleaded in a softer tone. "I don't understand. I'm tired of being afraid."

His chest spasmed with a rippling movement. And then she heard another sound. Laughter.

She'd admitted she was afraid of him, of his relentless torment, and that made him laugh. Hazel backed away from the mocking sound.

Big mistake, Dr. Coop. You just gave him what he wanted.

Part of what he wanted, at least. *Everything* probably involved a whole lot more than this mental anguish— like panic or torture. Or dying.

"Good," he dragged out in a toneless whisper. He pushed the button on the device in his hand and replaced the cover. *Off.* Then, with a single finger, he traced the outline of a metal link. Hazel shivered as she imagined him touching her skin with that same finger. "I'll take that as down payment on what you owe me."

She frowned. Why couldn't she recognize that voice? Or was she only imagining it sounded familiar?

She picked up Cleo, and for a split second she wished her little schnauzer was as well trained as Gunny. She'd order her dog to bite that stupid, creepily suggestive finger. She wished she had Burke's partner with her here right now to take him down and sink his teeth into him and chew that hideous mask right off his face. She wished she had Burke.

The blare of an approaching siren pulled Hazel from the violent turn of her thoughts and stiffened her spine. "You're caught."

He shook his head in a silent no. Then he picked up

the package and the dead cat and backed away from the gate as swirling lights from the first official vehicle bounced off the trees across the street.

"Wait!" Hazel dashed to the pedestrian exit as the man ran down the sidewalk, disappearing into the curtain of rain and night. If KCPD didn't catch him now, he'd be free to come back and taunt her again, to hurt someone else. One of her daughters? Her neighbors? Her coworkers and patients? His threats had already escalated to the point that she was certain he intended a messy death for her. But how many innocent people did his idea of *everything* include?

She shoved open the heavy door and ran outside into the rain. "You won't get away with this!" The sirens were deafening as the first official vehicle reached her block. She halted as rain splashed her face and soaked through her clothes. Cleo huddled against her as she peered through the distorted lights of emergency vehicles and streetlamps that highlighted individual raindrops instead of what lay beyond them. She couldn't even see the corner of the building, much less the man. She took one more step, and then another, following in a hesitant pursuit. "Don't run from me now! You're not so brave without a bomb to keep me in check, are you! I want to talk to—"

A big black-and-white pickup swerved into the parking ramp in front of her, screeching to a halt on the damp pavement. Hazel jumped back from the truck that blocked her path. "No!" She dodged around the truck, trying to get eyes on her tormentor. "He's getting away."

But she ran into a wall made of man and uniform.

"Hazel!" The KCPD truck was still rocking from its abrupt stop when Burke jumped out from behind the wheel. Leaving the engine running, he circled around the hood and locked his arm around her waist, catching her before she could dart past him. "What the hell are you doing out here?"

"Stop him!"

She shuffled in quick backward steps to stay upright as he pulled her up against the brick wall. "The only thing that kept me from going crazy imagining all the ways he could hurt you was knowing there was that cage between him and you."

She clung to a fistful of his jacket, even as she tried to slide around him. "He went that way. Around the corner. I didn't think it was safe to come out while he was still here. We need to catch—"

"It wasn't." Burke pushed his hips against hers, trapping her between him and the wall. Clearly, he wasn't letting her move away.

"Damn it, Burke." She pushed. Nothing happened. "I don't want to lose… I don't…" Her fingers slowly curled into his jacket and the vest, shirt and man underneath it. Had she never fully realized how tall and broad he was? She couldn't see anything beyond the expanse of his shoulders. And he was as immovable as the brick wall at her back. But her ebbing panic still wouldn't let her settle against him. "I don't want him to get away. He has a bomb. He'll hurt someone. He'll come back. We have to go after him."

"That's my job. Your safety is my priority." He

framed her jaw between his hands, tilting her face up to study her expression, stopping any chance of her putting herself in danger. "Are you okay?"

She calmed herself in the warmth and clarity of Burke's whiskey-brown eyes before nodding. "Cleo spotted him. I was walking her around the garage. He had a dead cat he put by the gate. Like bait to lure us to him. Then I saw the package, and the dog started barking and suddenly he was…" Her arm tightened around Cleo as she remembered the devilish mask and sightless eyes. Then she felt the stroke of Burke's thumb across her lips and came back to the present. Back to a warm body and fiercely protective expression. Back to the man who felt like her future.

If she could survive the present.

Hazel eased her grip on the front on his uniform, letting her hand settle over his heart. "He was right there. As close as you and I are now, with only that grating between us. Cleo was having a fit. I backed away and tried to keep him talking, to get him to stay after I texted you."

Burke rubbed Cleo's head. "Good girl. You were protecting your mama."

Feeling his praise of her feisty little schnauzer like a comforting caress to her own frayed nerves, she turned her head toward the curled-up paper on the other side of the gate. "There's another letter."

"Did you read it?"

Hazel nodded. "I didn't want to. But I thought it would keep him here until help arrived. It's like the others—creepy and obsessive. Only…I don't think it's about love. Having him here made it feel like this is all about revenge."

"Revenge for what?"

Hazel shrugged and shook her head. "This isn't some unrequited crush like I thought it was at first. He's…angry at me. I don't know why. He wants to punish me."

Burke started to pull her into his arms, but, with a dog between them and a second and third black-and-white pulling up behind his truck, he ended up sliding his palm to the back of her neck and briefly massaging the sensitive skin at her nape instead. As he stepped back, she noticed the flashing lights of a fourth KCPD car blocking the intersection at the end of the street. Another vehicle was pulling into place at the opposite end of the block to stop traffic, while a SWAT van pulled into the parking lot across the street.

"You rallied the troops."

"We take bomb threats very seriously." He feathered his fingertips through the fringe of hair at her nape, sending a trickle of much-needed warmth through her. "I take protecting *you* very seriously."

She reached up to wind her fingers around the damp sleeve clinging to his sturdy forearm, thanking him. "I know. And I know you want to be more than just a protection detail. Part of me wants that, too. But I need you to understand the kind of baggage I come with if we pursue this relationship."

His eyes darkened with interest. "That's a conversation I want to have. But I need to be a cop right now. Later. Okay?"

"Okay."

"Sergeant Burke?" Two uniformed officers, wearing plastic ponchos and KCPD ball caps, appeared at his shoulder.

Burke blinked and the heat in his eyes had vanished. The veteran police sergeant had replaced the man she loved. He slipped his hand to the more neutral position of her shoulder and turned to the two young men. "The perp ran toward Broadway a few minutes ago. Black hoodie. Dark jeans. Halloween mask. See if you can get eyes on him but keep your distance. Chances are he's carrying a bomb."

"Yes, sir." The officers ran down the block, splitting up to cover both sides of the street.

She recognized the next cop, Justin Grant, who moved in beside Burke. His green eyes swept over her face. "Dr. Coop okay?"

Burke pushed her toward the lanky blond man before releasing his grip on her. "She stays with you. She doesn't leave your sight." He glanced down at her before giving orders to Justin. "Give your statement to Bellamy and Cartwright when they get here. Take her upstairs. I'll radio if I find anything."

Burke hesitated for a moment, tension radiating off his body, seeming uncharacteristically unsure of his next move. His reluctance to leave her to pursue the suspect reminded Hazel of the independent strength that had sustained her for more than sixteen years. She loved him for his concern but understood that the best way for him to catch her stalker and would-be bomber who could harm so many more people was to assure him she could draw on that strength and be okay without him.

She reached around Cleo to splay her hand at the center of his chest. "Go. Do your job. Gunny will have your back." She curled her fingers into the front of his jacket and stretched up to press a quick kiss to his mouth. Then she pulled away and looked up at Burke's friend. "Justin will have mine."

With his dark gaze never leaving hers, he nodded. Then he hunched his shoulders against the rain and jogged to his truck.

She heard Gunny whining with excitement as Burke grabbed the big dog's leash from the front. When he opened the back door, the Czech shepherd was dancing at the edge of his cage.

"You keep an eye on him, Gunny!" she called out.

"Come on, boy." Burke hooked up his partner and the shepherd jumped down beside him. "You got one more job in you today?" Gunny looked up at him, his tail wagging in anticipation, waiting for the command to go to work. "Gunny, *Fuss!*"

They moved off at a quick pace, following the devil man and the other two officers down the street.

Hazel watched the rainy night swallow up man and dog, trotting off to do battle with a bomb and the monster who wanted her dead.

Chapter Ten

Hazel startled when she felt Justin's hand at her elbow. "The old man said to get you inside, and I do what the boss says."

"He'll be all right, won't he?" Hazel punched in the code to unlock the door to the pedestrian entrance to the parking garage. "I want him to be focused on his own safety, not me."

"This neighborhood is swarming with cops right now," Justin promised. "He's not alone in some kind of *High Noon* face-off against this guy."

"But it's so dark out there. The streetlights won't do anyone much good until the rain lets up. I didn't see him until he was practically on top of me." A fist squeezed around her heart at all the worst-case scenarios that suddenly filled her head. "A bomb and... that man...can do a lot of damage."

Justin followed her inside, locking the door behind him. "It sounds odd, but the best eyes out there are Gunny's nose. He'll smell a threat long before Burke or anyone else sees it."

"All those men and women who showed up—they

aren't in Burke's chain of command, are they?" Hazel asked. "I know you're not."

Justin's grin took the edge off her concern. "I don't know anyone on the force who doesn't move when Sergeant Burke says jump. And we've been doing a lot of jumping lately."

"Because of me?"

"It's not like we don't all owe him for one favor or another. He and his dogs have saved more of our hides than we can count." Justin took off his cap and smacked it against his thigh to remove the excess water before slipping it back over his blond hair. "Besides, it's about time he found something to care about besides work and dog training. It put an end to those awkward conversations with my wife, asking me to introduce him to one of her friends because she's worried about him turning into a lonely old man. I keep telling her he's one of that rare breed of man who'd rather be alone than with the wrong woman." He winked. "I'd bet money that you're the right one."

The right one. Burke would rather be alone than with someone besides her. Something warmed deep inside Hazel, even as she shivered at the pressure that pronouncement put on her vow to remain single and protect herself from getting hurt again. Did everyone in Kansas City except for her know how long Burke had had feelings for her?

"I'm not sure I'm the best choice for him."

"He's decided what he needs. He doesn't do dumb or boring, and he doesn't do disloyal." Justin pulled a plastic evidence bag from a pocket in his jacket. "I'm sure you know how hard it is for him to trust after the hell his ex-wife put him through."

Hazel bristled at the mention of his ex. She admitted there was a tad of jealousy behind her tense reaction. Shannon Bennett had once owned Jedediah's heart. She'd been in his bed and had most likely been shielded from the nightmares the world threw at her by Burke's broad shoulders and protective instincts. He'd probably made her laugh and had shared intimate conversations and given her knee-melting kisses—all those things she could no longer deny that she wanted for herself. But mostly, she couldn't fathom how anyone would willingly hurt the good man she cared for so much.

"I know she cheated on him."

Justin snorted through his nose. "Wasn't just once. Every time he deployed, she made a new friend." Hazel's heart squeezed with anger, but Justin continued as though he was discussing the inclement weather. He knelt beside the curled letter and envelope. "A man likes to be needed, but it's also nice to know your woman can handle it if you're not there 24-7. It's probably why he likes his dogs so much. They're loyal down to the bone."

Was that how Burke saw her? As an independent woman who was also a loyal friend? With all the problems she'd had in her marriage, at least infidelity hadn't been an issue she'd gone through with Aaron. And even after everything had crashed and burned, she'd never considered being unfaithful to her vows. Of course, she hadn't been willing to trust any man enough to seek out a new relationship. Not until Jedediah Burke had walked into her vet clinic. She understood that she was the woman Burke wanted. But could she truly be the woman he needed? Did she have it in her to give him the kind of love and mutual trust that he deserved?

Thankfully, Justin switched his focus from her relationship with Burke back to the investigation. When the bomb squad officer pulled out a multiuse tool and opened a tweezers attachment to pick up the letter, Hazel pointed out that the man in the Halloween mask had worn gloves. "You won't get any prints from those."

"We'll let the lab be the judge of that." He slipped the letter and envelope into a bag and sealed it. "I want them to check for explosives residue. That can be as much of a signature in tracking down this guy as any prints." Once he towered over her again, he walked her to the elevator and pushed the call button. "Let's go."

On the way up the elevator, Justin jotted the date and location on the evidence bag. He read the message on the letter and muttered an expletive. "This guy's a piece of work. No wonder Burke has been working overtime to get a lead on him. Can you tell me anything about the package?"

Hazel absentmindedly scratched Cleo between her ears. Exhaustion was quickly claiming her now that the adrenaline spike of her stalker's visit was wearing off. "I never saw inside it. It was shaped like a long shoebox. Wrapped in brown paper. Addressed to me. He took it with him."

When they reached the fourth floor, Hazel set Cleo down and unlocked the door to her condo.

"Hold up." After flipping the dead bolt, Justin asked her to wait beside the door. Just as Burke had for the past two nights, the younger officer moved through each room of her apartment, checking under beds and in closets, securing every window and the fire escape exit before coming back to her at the front door. "Everything looks good. You can relax."

Right. Relax. That was still a work in progress. She was keenly aware of the difference between fatigue and feeling relaxed.

But out loud, she thanked Justin for his presence. "Thanks." She unhooked Cleo's leash, and the dog trotted into the kitchen to lap up a big drink of water. Hazel kicked off her shoes on the mat beside the door and peeled off her wet jacket before following the dog to the kitchen. She rinsed out the coffeepot and started a fresh brew before she heard Justin pulling out one of the stools behind her.

"Burke said you got pictures of the perp and the package." His tone was friendly enough, but also like Burke, he was all business when it came to the investigation. "Show me."

Hazel pulled her phone from the pocket of her jeans and set it on the island counter for him to look through. "You can't tell anything just by looking at the picture, can you?"

"You'd be surprised. The key to finding an unknown bomber is to identify his signature—the way he builds his device, the components he chooses." Justin scrolled through the pictures. "For example, how did he pick up the package when he left? Did he move slowly? Make a point of keeping it parallel to the ground?"

Hazel hugged her arms around her sticky T-shirt and realized she was soaked to the skin. That didn't help the chill she was feeling. She looked beyond Justin to the bank of windows and wondered how wet Burke and Gunny were. If they were cold. Tired. If they were facing down the devil-faced man. She'd hear an explosion, either accidentally or intentionally detonated, at this distance, even with the storm muffling the city noises outside, wouldn't she?

"He'll be okay. Gunny won't let anybody hurt him," Justin said. She dragged her focus back to him as he set his cap on the counter and continued as if she hadn't just gone to a very dark place in her head. "Now, tell me about the package itself."

"You're trying to distract me, so I don't worry about Jedediah."

He arched a golden eyebrow. "Is it working?"

"No. Still worried." She summoned a half smile to match his. "But I can multitask." The chocolatey, earthy scent of coffee filled the kitchen as she pulled down two mugs and poured them each a cup. "The man grabbed the box by one end and tucked it under his arm like a football." She replayed the memory of the man's blank eyeholes and labored breathing as he disappeared into the rain. "He ran. As fast as his huffing and puffing would let him."

Justin turned down her offer of cream and sugar and took a drink, barely giving the coffee time to cool. "Then it's not motion activated like most pipe bombs are. More likely, he set it to detonate with a cell phone where he can call in and set it off exactly when he wants. Thrill bombers often use that setup— they want to witness the destruction they cause, but from a safe distance."

A shiver crawled across Hazel's skin at the grue-some image that created. "Like an addict? Only his drug of choice is blowing things up?"

"Exactly."

She remembered the stroke of his thumb over the electronic device in her stalker's gloved hand. "Wait a minute." She picked up her phone and scrolled through the pictures before pointing one blurry image out to Justin. "It's not a great picture, but he held a device in his hand. He kept saying he was turning it on and off. I kept thinking he was going to detonate the bomb then and there."

"A kill switch."

Hazel shivered. "That sounds ominous."

"He was arming and disarming the weapon. That tells me a lot." Justin set her cell aside to text some notes into his own phone. "He might have been using a timer. Stopping the countdown to continue the conversation—or forcing you to do what he wanted." He'd wanted her to read the letter. He'd wanted her to know that he was in complete control of whether she lived or died. Hazel sank onto the stool beside Justin as he talked through his thoughts out loud. "Although starting and stopping the countdown like that would be like playing Russian roulette. A faulty disconnect or losing track of the countdown would put him right there if the bomb went off. He might have some kind of suicide scenario going on in his head—like the two of you ending together. He probably wouldn't want an audience of police officers, though, if that was the case. It would depersonalize the event too much for him. Unless it wasn't a bomb at all." He glanced down over his shoulder at her. "But another fake meant to terrorize you."

Thrill bombers? Kill switches? Suicide scenarios? This winking, easygoing man had a disturbing knowledge of explosive devices and all the ways her stalker could kill her. Not to mention the knowledge to disarm the devices himself. "Your wife must be a very brave woman, considering all the risks you take."

He nodded. "The bravest. Did you know that Emilia helped me with an undercover op when we first started dating? Of course, I accidentally forced her into it."

"Accidentally?"

His cheeks turned slightly pink. With regret? Embarrassment? A remembered heat? "My mission had gone sideways. I needed her to bail me out. She was brilliant."

While Justin told her the story of how he and his doctor wife had met in an emergency room, and a kiss to keep her from exposing his cover had led to taking down a serial bomber and eventually to marriage and starting a family, Hazel heated up soup and made sandwiches for Justin, Burke and herself. Then she changed into dry clothes and set out coffee mugs and towels for the officers who were coming up to interview her. She made a quick call to each of her daughters. Polly told her about Garrett Cho, the police officer who'd been assigned to watch their apartment. Ashley was still on her date with Joe Sciarra, who got on the phone himself to assure her that he'd keep an eye on Ash and would take her home ASAP. And though she didn't doubt that the muscular bouncer could defend himself and her older daughter, it was hard for Hazel to let either of her girls out of her sight—even knowing they were both grown, responsible young women.

Almost an hour passed before Hazel heard a knock on her door and sloshed her tepid coffee over the rim of her mug. Unlike the two detectives she'd buzzed in earlier, she'd given Burke the pass code to get into her building, so she knew he could come straight up to her condo. But still, she jumped at the unexpected sound. Justin was on his feet, his hand on the butt of his gun at his waist, crossing to the door, before Burke announced himself. "It's me, Haze. Tell Justin to let me in."

By the time Justin unlocked the door, Hazel had grabbed a clean towel and was crossing the room.

"Heads up on the muddy paw prints," Burke warned. "Gunny, *sitz*—"

"It's okay." Gunny zipped past her, leaving a trail

across the hardwood floor and area rug in front of the couch as he greeted Cleo, and the two dogs sniffed and curled up together on the blanket she'd left out for the working dog. Hazel shook the towel loose and patted the moisture from Burke's face and neck. "Let him warm up and relax. Gunny's okay, right?"

"He's fine."

"And you?"

Burke carried his gear bag in one hand and held out a wilted paper sack in the other. His pants were caked with mud up to his knees and the scruff of his beard was dotted with droplets of water. "I'm afraid dinner's cold and wet. So am I."

Hazel didn't care. She tossed the towel across his shoulders and slid her arms around his waist, walking into his chest. While the dampness of his clothes seeped into hers, she aligned her body with his, tucked her head beneath his chin and squeezed him tight, saying nothing until she detected the warmth of his body and felt a deep sigh roll through his chest. She heard the double thunk of him dropping both bags and breathed her own sigh of relief when his strong arms folded around her.

"I'm drippin' on you, Doc." His voice was a husky growl against her ear.

"Just let me hold you for a minute."

"I've got no problem with that. But I'm fine, Haze." He stepped to one side, pulling her with him as Justin locked the door behind him. "Any issues here?" he asked the officer who'd been guarding her.

Justin shook his head. "The detectives took her

statement. Dr. Coop let me rattle on about Emilia, the kids and me."

"You're good at talking," Burke teased. "I'm surprised you didn't put her to sleep with the way you go on sometimes."

"Would you be serious?" Hazel swatted his backside beneath his gun belt before hugging him at his waist again. "Most people run away from a bomb. You and Gunny ran right toward it. Justin was trying to keep me from freaking out."

"Freak out? Cool-in-a-Crisis Cooper?" His arms tightened around her. "Never gonna happen."

The nylon of his jacket was cold against her cheek. But where her forehead rested against the skin of his neck, she felt the strong, warm beat of his pulse. He was joking with his friend. Teasing her. All normal stuff. He was in one piece. He was okay. She was okay, too, now that she could see and feel his strength and steady demeanor for herself. As the tension that had been building inside her eased to a level much more manageable than freak-out mode, the need to be practical and stay busy seeped back in. Hazel stepped back and removed Burke's soggy cap, hanging it on the coat rack beside the door before pulling open the snaps of his jacket and pushing it off his shoulders. "He got away, didn't he?"

He waited for her to hang up his jacket before answering. "He must have had a vehicle waiting and drove off before we set up the blockade. Gunny lost his scent." Burke held himself still and let her tend him, as though he sensed how badly she needed to do something to help stop the man stalking her, even if all she could do was keep the officers working the case warm and dry. She unzipped Burke's vest and discovered the clothes underneath were just as wet. But when she unhooked his belt and lifted its heavy weight, he took it from her hands and set it on his bag beside him. Then he untucked his uniform shirt and T-shirt and took over the drying job. "Did you call the girls? Are they okay?"

Restless with nothing to do but wonder at the truth and worry, Hazel retrieved a stool from the kitchen so that Burke could sit and take off his boots. "Polly's at home. There's an Officer Cho outside her building."

"Cho's a good man." Burke tousled his brown-and-gray hair into short spikes with the towel. "The boyfriend's not there with them, is he?"

Alarm surged anew through her, and she plunked the stool down with a bang. "No. Joe and Ashley aren't home yet. Why? Did you find out something about him? Joe talked like a bodyguard—like you do sometimes. He promised to watch over her and take her home. She'll call as soon as she's there. Do you have a bad vibe about him?"

His brown eyes locked on to hers. "I've got a bad vibe about anybody I haven't personally vetted who comes in contact with the Cooper women."

Dialing her panic back a notch at his stern assertion, she knelt to untie his boots. "So nothing specific. That's good."

"Maybe not," Burke admitted. "The only Joseph Sciarra I found in the system was sixty years old.

No way was the guy on that motorcycle with Ashley sixty. I was expanding my name search when you sent me that first text."

"Could Joe be a nickname?" Hazel asked, hating the idea of a man lying to her daughter more than she hated the stiff, muddy laces of Burke's boots soiling her hands.

"It's a possibility. It could also be something as innocent as him using an alias for his bouncer job. That way, unhappy customers can't track him down after hours if he had to toss them out or call the cops on them." Burke hung his vest on the hook beside his jacket. "I plan to have a conversation with him tomorrow."

"Do I need to call Ashley again?"

"And tell her what?" He pried off his boot and set it on the drip mat beside the door. "Joe can't be the man who was here talking to you because he's been with her all evening. Right?"

Of course. That made logical sense. Her stalker couldn't be in two places at the same time—and she *had* talked to Joe on Ashley's phone. Hazel nodded. She pressed her lips into a wry smile. "I'm the mom here. I shouldn't scare her more than I already have. I guess it's hard for me to trust any man right now."

His fingers cupped beneath her chin to tilt her face up to his. "Any man?"

She rolled her eyes toward the living room, where Justin was reporting the information he and Burke had gathered to another member of his team. She squeezed her fingers around Burke's wrist and smiled. "With a few notable exceptions."

"Glad I made the short list." He stroked his thumb across her lips in that ticklish caress that made things inside her curl with anticipation before releasing her. "If we don't hear from Ashley in an hour or so, telling us she's safely home with Polly and Garrett Cho, we'll call her then."

"Deal." She moved on to the next muddy boot. "What about you? The devil man didn't threaten you, did he?"

"The devil man?"

"The Halloween mask he wore. I saw it up close tonight."

"Like he needs a nickname. No. I never got eyes on him. Just that damn picture you sent me." He pulled her to her feet in front of him. His hands settled at her waist, his fingers kneading an unspoken message into the skin beneath the sweatshirt she wore. "Are you sure you're not hurt or in shock? What did he say to spook you like this?"

The man's words hadn't been as cutting as his laughter. She'd rebelled against his threats and cryptic pronouncements. But his laughter had crippled her like the blows she'd suffered the night Aaron's friend had tried to silence her. If she hadn't been a veterinarian…if she hadn't had her bag and the syringe and the tranquilizer with her…

Her attacker that night had laughed, too. Right up until he felt the needle she'd jabbed into his thigh.

The next day, when she left the hospital, she'd gone

straight to the DA's office and told him she was ready to testify against her husband. She'd seen her attorney about divorce proceedings by the end of the same day.

"Haze?" Burke's callused fingers brushed the bangs across her forehead before settling beneath her chin and tilting her face up to his. "You're scaring me a little bit. Tell me what happened."

"Nothing new." She glanced over her shoulder at Justin and used his presence as an excuse to keep her humiliating secrets a little while longer. Mustering a weak smile, she slipped from his grasp. "Exhausted beyond belief, but I'm not hurt." His eyes narrowed with a question she felt too raw to answer. Instead, she smoothed his wild hair into some semblance of order and carried the wet towel to the pile beside the laundry closet off the kitchen. "The coffee's hot. Want a cup?" Not waiting for an answer, she poured him a mug. From the kitchen she heard the thud of the second boot hit the mat. "At least he took the bomb with him, right? If that's what it was."

The next thing she heard was the deep rumble of his voice beside her. "The makings of one, anyway. Gunny hit on the spot by the gate." He took the mug from her trembling hands, tested the temperature and took a long swallow of the strong black brew.

Justin strolled into the kitchen, reminding her they weren't alone. "That confirms there were explosives. I've got Dr. Coop's statement, some decent pics and a pretty good idea of the type of bomb this guy builds. I'll file the report. You good here?"

With a nod, Burke set down the coffee and walked his friend to the door. "I got this. Thanks, Justin."

The two men shook hands. "You need anything, call. Cartwright and Bellamy said they'd post a unit outside once they're done canvasing the neighborhood and taking witness statements. They've explained what to look for to the man watching your daughters' apartment, too. Dark hoodie. Halloween mask. Brown paper packages—and not the good kind."

"I owe you one." Burke opened the door.

"You owe me nothing, old man. You and that mutt have kept my team alive more than once. It's about time you let me return the favor." Justin pulled his KCPD cap over his head and tipped the brim to Hazel. "Dr. Coop."

"Thank you for everything."

The younger man winked and strode into the hallway. Burke set the dead bolt behind him and turned to face Hazel across the main room. "I need a hot shower, and Gunny needs food and rest."

In other words, he needed her to take care of herself for a few minutes. He needed her to be more than his ex-wife had ever been for him.

She summoned the dregs of her depleted strength and went to work. "I'll fix you a plate of food and take care of Gunny while you change. If you leave your clothes in the laundry basket, I can run them through the wash, too."

Instead of nodding or speaking, or any other response she might have expected, Burke strode into the kitchen, clasped her face between his hands and lowered his mouth to hers. With nothing more than his fingers in her hair and his lips moving over hers, he kissed her very, very thoroughly. Desire sparked inside her, leaping to meet his claim. Hazel rose up onto her toes, pushing her mouth into his kiss. Her lips parted, welcoming him. Her tongue darted out to meet his, and she tasted coffee and a frantic need that matched her own. She clutched at the front of his shirt, then crawled her fingers up into the damp spikes of his hair. Her hips hit the countertop as Burke's muscular thighs crowded against hers. His kiss permeated her body with a transfusion of heat. The faint desperation and sure claim of his mouth jolted through her heart. Her frayed emotions healed beneath the sweep of his tongue and the press of his body and the needy grasp of his hands.

This was what she needed. The touch of this good man. This celebration of life. Jedediah Burke erased the loneliness from her life. He shared her burdens and made her pulse race and her heart smile. He made her feel as though the emotional isolation that had protected her for so long was a mistake—that she could live more fully, love more completely in a way she hadn't allowed herself to for too many years.

But almost as resolutely as the kiss had begun, Burke pulled away with a ragged sigh. He rested his lips against her forehead for a moment, and she felt the heat of their kiss dissipating into the cool skin there.

"I needed to do that earlier," he confessed. "I was so damn scared that he was going to hurt you." He leaned back, brushing aside her bangs with his fingertips to study her expression. His chest heaved in a deep breath that showed far more control than the mewling gasps she could currently muster. "You sure you're okay?"

Where had the man learned to kiss like that? And now that she'd tasted the depths of Burke's passion, she was becoming addicted to every touch they shared. She felt weak yet energized, totally confused and absolutely right. "Is it too sappy to say I'm better now?"

He gave a slight laugh. "Then count me on the sappy side, too." But his handsome, weary expression was dead serious. "You've been acting a little weird since I got here. Did Justin say something that upset you? The detectives?"

Hazel fiddled with collar of his damp T-shirt before meeting his gaze. "I'm keeping it together for now, okay? Let's just leave it at that."

"Doc, you know you can tell me anything. About the case, that emotional baggage you mentioned earlier—anything."

"I know. I will," she promised. "But first things first." She turned him and nudged him down the hallway. "Go. Before you catch a cold. Or else I'll be worried about you all over again. And the only meds I have on hand are for canines."

When he hesitated at the bathroom doorway, she gave him another gentle push. But this time he didn't budge. "I'm not laughing, Haze. Are you sure you're okay?"

She shrugged, giving him an honest answer. "I just need a little time to myself to process…everything. My life is changing, and I need to make sure I'm making the right decisions."

"Fair enough," he answered, understanding that *he* was one of those decisions. He remembered his bag at the front door and retrieved it. "I usually take a quick shower. Do you need me to linger? Give you more time?"

She shook her head. "Take however long you need. I'll step in after I hear the water running to get your dirty clothes."

Five minutes later, with the shower running and Burke humming a sweetly tuneless song, Hazel's decision was made. She hadn't been whole before Burke strode into her life five years ago with his first K-9 partner. There was a reason she'd turned to him when she'd been afraid of those letters. A reason she worried about the dangers he faced on her behalf and to protect Kansas City. A reason she'd never considered giving her heart and her soul and her kisses to another man.

She loved Jedediah Burke, loved him with a fierce intensity that was as frightening as it was exciting.

She'd been surviving for a long, long time. But she hadn't been living. She couldn't preach to her daughters to embrace life and love hard and trust a good man if she wouldn't do the same for herself. Jedediah was her partner in every way that mattered.

Except one.

Chapter Eleven

Hazel tapped softly on the bathroom door and waited for Burke's invitation before pushing it open. A cloud of steamy, fragrant air filtered past as she entered the room to open the clothes hamper. As the steam rushed out of the enclosed space, she spotted Burke's bag in the corner beside the sink, his open Dopp kit sitting on the counter.

But with his damp clothes hugged to her chest, she froze, her gaze transfixed by the blurry outline of Burke's tall, muscular form through the mottled glass of the walk-in shower door. He'd stopped moving, too. He must have been rinsing his hair or easing the tightness of overworked muscles by letting the hot water sluice over his neck and shoulders. His body was arched forward, his strong arms braced against the tile wall, his head bowed into the pelting spray of water. Even though she couldn't make out a clear visual image, her brain was cataloging every detail. The sprinkles of silver in his dark brown hair. The breadth of his arms and shoulders. The graceful arch of his long back and curved buttocks. The spicy scents of soap and man, and the earthier scents of grit and sweat washing down the drain teased her nose. Something purely female clenched with a sensual awareness deep inside her. Something unexpectedly protective and faintly territorial squeezed at her heart, too.

She was a veterinarian doctor, for Pete's sake. She knew all about anatomy, both human and animal. She'd been married once a lifetime ago. But there was nothing clinical to her reaction to Burke showering in her home, nothing naive about this connection flowing like a strong current between them whenever they got close. This was how her life could be, how it should have been all along, if only she'd loved this man first.

The way she loved him now.

Burke shook his head, then shifted position behind the translucent glass, reaching for the washcloth he'd tossed over the top of the door. "Sorry about the mud. I'll clean up in here. You may have to wash those pants by themselves."

Hazel dropped the dirty clothes she held. She needed to do this. Now.

"My ex-husband…Aaron…" She inhaled a steadying breath of the tiny room's humid air to quell the terrifying memories that rose like bile in her throat. "Sixteen years ago, Aaron paid a man to kill me. To stop me from testifying against him."

Burke's curse was pithy and succinct. Movement stopped behind the glass, although the sound of the water beating down on the tiles at his feet never ceased. "I know I promised we'd talk, but you couldn't have eased into that?"

This was already like ripping a bandage from raw skin. She'd started, and now the past was oozing out like the festering wound it was. Besides, it was easier to share the truth without Burke's dark eyes probing into hers, seeing more than anyone else ever had.

She needed to say this. She needed to say all of it. She needed Burke to know why she was such a hot mess in the relationship department. "He hired a friend of his—a man who worked for him on and off at the investment firm. Aaron used the money I'd stashed away in an account for the girls to pay him. Out in the country—I was on my way to an emergency call. A dog had been hit, left to die on the side of the road." She wanted to laugh at the prophetic analogy but had never been able to. "Maybe the dog was already dead. Maybe it never existed. Aaron took the call that night. The judge hadn't seized our house as an asset yet, so we were still living together. Separate rooms, but his lawyer said it helped Aaron's image for the press and jury to think we were still a couple, that he still had my support. He knew the DA had been talking to me."

"Aaron set you up." Burke's posture changed behind the glass, from weary like a man at the end of a long day to alert like the cop he was. He quickly rinsed off. "I want to hear all of it."

"I never saw the headlights until they were right on me. He rammed his car into mine. Rolled me into the ditch."

Burke shut off the water and reached for the towel outside the shower door.

"Because of my seat belt and air bags, I didn't die in the accident. But I was pretty shaken up, a little disoriented when I climbed out through the broken window. I knew Aaron's friend. I thought he was there to save me. That he'd stopped to help. I was so grateful. I was asking if he'd seen the dog who'd been hit. Then he smashed my head against the side of the car. He used his fists and his feet to try to finish the job."

Biting down on a string of curses, Burke stepped out of the shower, knotting the towel at his hips. "Hazel..."

When he reached for her, she took a step back, hugging her arms around her waist. He retreated to the bath mat, perhaps sensing how brittle she felt, how she'd shatter into a thousand pieces if anyone touched her right now. It was probably killing him to refrain from taking action, not to be able to fix this for her.

Instead, he raked his fingers through his wet hair. "I know there's more." His voice was tight, deep. "You're here now. Tell me how you survived."

She zeroed in on the oval pucker of his belly button, linked by a line of dark hair down to the knot on his towel. His stomach was flat, his skin beaded with moisture and flushed with a heat that radiated across the room; his muscles were taut beneath that skin. But what turned her on the most was that stellar control, that endless patience that made her feel she could share everything with him. He respected her need to fight her way through her past, to approach this relationship at the speed she needed to go. Caked with mud, dog hair and layers of protective uniform, or practically naked as the day he was born, Burke wasn't just the man she wanted—he was the man she needed.

She lifted her gaze to his whiskey-brown eyes and found them studying her just as intently as she'd expected. "Aaron's friend laughed at me. He sounded crazy. Drunk? High? I don't know. He joked about refunding the money. Said the job was too easy. He was putting me back in the car, buckling me in, telling me how he was going to set it on fire and blame my death on the accident. Once I was inside, I could reach my bag. I had a syringe with a tranquilizer already loaded. In case the dog didn't cooperate. I stabbed him with it. He passed out before I did. I called the police. I don't remember anything more until I woke up in the ambulance."

"That's the Hazel Cooper I know. You used your head and you fought back." He relaxed the fists that had clenched at his sides. "Is that when you decided to testify against your ex?"

"Murder for hire and attempted murder got Aaron a lot longer sentence than the fraud and embezzlement alone would have."

He took a step forward and she didn't bolt. "And the hit man he hired?"

"The tranquilizer I gave him must have reacted with whatever was already in his system. The paramedics couldn't revive him."

Burke's fingers tiptoed across the top of the vanity

and brushed against her elbow. Hazel didn't flinch. If anything, she shifted slightly to the left, moving her elbow into the cup of his hand. She'd just admitted that she'd killed a man—but she saw no recrimination in his eyes, felt no pity in his touch. "You weren't charged, were you?"

She shook her head. "Evidence at the scene and Aaron's money trail made it a clear case of self-defense. My testimony gave the DA the victory he wanted. It ultimately doubled Aaron's sentence."

Burke drifted a half step closer, feathering his fingertips into her bangs, brushing them off her forehead. "I've never met your ex, have I?"

Despite the gentleness of his caress, tension coiled beneath each syllable.

"I doubt it. I filed every restraining order in the book to keep him away from Ashley, Polly and me." She shrugged. "He calls me sometimes." The soothing caresses stopped. Hazel reached up to capture Burke's hand against her cheek. "I don't answer. The girls barely remember him. Polly probably wouldn't even recognize him. She was so young when he went away."

He simply nodded as if some sort of truce had been reached. "Do you think your ex is behind this terror campaign?"

"I don't know. It could be Aaron, wanting to punish me for my *betrayal*. It could be someone else he hired."

"I'll follow up on his whereabouts since his release from prison." He stroked his thumb across her lips before pulling away. "What do you need from me right now?"

There was nowhere to retreat in the small room. And Hazel didn't want him to. "I just needed you to listen. I need you to understand why I've put you off for so many years and insisted that friendship was enough."

Lines deepened beside his eyes as he paused. "You want us to go back to being just friends?"

"No." She touched her fingertips to the worry grooves on his rugged face and willed them to relax. "I think you and I are destined to be something more. But I want you to understand that because of everything I went through, I've had a really hard time trusting men over the years. I gave my heart to a man who thought killing me was a better choice than admitting his guilt and giving us a chance to repair our fractured marriage. I trusted that we could at least have an amicable divorce and still both have a hand in raising our girls. How smart does that make me about relationships?"

She was the one drifting closer now, wanting to reassure him. She ran her fingers over the ticklish scruff of his beard, then drew them down his neck and across the jut of his shoulder.

"I know you're nothing like Aaron. But the doubts about myself have always been there. I never dealt with them because, frankly, I had a life I had to live. Children to raise, a practice to build. It's always been easier to bury my emotions than to deal with them. But you make me think about what I feel, what I want and need. I'm afraid of losing everything again. I want to be braver than I am. For you. For us. But—"

He caught her hand and raised it to his lips, pressing a warm kiss against her knuckles. "You are the bravest woman I know. You defended yourself against a man who wanted you dead. You kept your head in the face of danger. You lived your life in the way you needed to, so that you wouldn't be hurt again. And look at all the animals, all the people you've helped along the way. You have the right the live the way you need to, to choose who you want to have be a part of your life, to live—"

"I choose *you*." She took Burke's hands and placed them on either side of her waist. His fingers kneaded her skin beneath her sweatshirt but stayed resolutely where she'd put them. His nostrils flared with a ragged breath. Hazel felt the same warring need to skip the necessary words and get on with the physical connection they both craved as she braced her hands against his chest. "I want you to be a part of my life. But I'm scared I won't be any good at *us*, and I never want to hurt you."

Her thumb might have hooked around the turgid male nipple she discovered beneath the crisp curls of chest hair. His pectoral muscle might have jerked in a helpless response. But he fought for restraint until she'd said everything she wanted him to hear.

"Haze—"

"What if I can't make you happy? I know I try your patience. Why on earth would you want to be with a woman who runs hot and cold and smells like dog poop and antiseptic? Well, not all the time."

A low, guttural sound rumbled in his throat. "You make me laugh. And I didn't do enough of that until I met you. I have more in common with you than anyone I've ever known. Except maybe Gunny."

It was her turn to laugh. "I didn't do enough of that until I met you, either."

"You have sexy hair and the sweetest mouth." His fingers dipped inside the waistband of her jeans. "And a sexy, round—"

"I've given birth to two babies." She wasn't out of shape for a woman her age, but she *was* a woman of a certain age. "I eat too many sweets, and I haven't been with a man in years. *Years*, Jedediah."

"And I'm on the stud-of-the-month calendar?"

"You should be." She framed his strong jaw between her hands and admired the contours of every well-earned line beside his eyes, the firm shape of his mouth and the angle of his nose. He wasn't perfectly handsome, but she couldn't describe him as anything other than perfectly masculine. "You'd get my vote."

He squeezed his eyes shut for several seconds before his dark lashes fluttered open and his eyes looked their fill of her face, as she'd just studied his. "Do you know how badly I want to be with you?"

Hazel nodded. Years and doubts slipped away beneath the heat in his eyes. "I *want* to be with you. Help me heal. Please."

He lost the battle a split second before she did. His hands clamped around her bottom, snapping her to him, but Hazel was already sliding her arms around his neck. She palmed the back of his prickly wet hair and tilted his mouth down to hers. Their lips clashed like waves against a rocky shore. Tongues danced together, retreated like the ebbing tide, rushed in again. Hazel poured her heart into every tug, every taste. She clutched at his scalp, dug her fingers into the supple muscles of his back.

Just like that wild ocean current, the pain rushed out as desire swept in. Her nipples tightened and her breasts grew heavy with the friction of Burke's chest moving against hers. His hands slipped beneath her shirt, each sure stroke across her skin stirring the storm building inside her. He broke the kiss only long enough to whisk the shirt off over her head. And then his lips were back, grazing the tender skin along her neck, arousing eager nerve endings with the ticklish scratch of his beard, soothing them with the warm rasp of his tongue.

Her jeans felt rough between her legs as the pressure built inside her. She was keenly aware of the front of his towel tenting between them. *Too many clothes. Not enough skin.* Had she ever felt this hot? This demanding of a lover? This powerful? As Burke's mouth blazed a trail over the swell of her breast, she skimmed her hands down the length of his spine to reach the barrier of the damp towel at his hips. She inhaled the spicy scent of his warm skin before she nipped at the column of his neck, eliciting a growl from his throat. "Please tell me I haven't scared you off."

"Nope." His mouth closed, hot and wet, over the proud tip of her breast, pulling it into his mouth through the lace of her bra. Hazel gasped at the arrow of heat that shot straight to the needy heart of her. "All I heard was that you choose me. You want me. Do you have any idea how long I've been waiting to hear that?"

"About as long as I've wanted to say it?"

"I feel closer to you now than I ever have." He moved his attentions to the other breast, and she twisted against him, wanting even more. "Trust is a precious gift. And yours is hard to earn. Knowing I have it—for this—for everything—makes me want you even more."

"Jedediah…"

"Yes?"

Her hand fisted in the towel. "Too many clothes." She tugged.

He sought her mouth with his own and they laughed together as the towel landed at his feet, baring that fine, tight rump to the squeeze of her hands.

As smoothly as she'd rid him of a simple towel, he unsnapped her jeans and pushed them and her panties down over her hips. The bra went next and then he caught her behind the knee to pull her to him, rocking against her core, driving all kinds of delicious pressure into the most sensitive of places inside her. The hard length of him pressing against her told her he was just as ready as she.

"Protection?" he growled against her skin.

Hazel gasped out a curse. "I haven't been on the

pill in years. Of course, I haven't needed to be. I don't know if the girls left—"

He silenced the moment of panic with a hard kiss. "Not a problem. Pants?"

"By the hamper. I haven't had a chance—"

He turned her and swatted her bottom. "I'll meet you in the bedroom."

He retrieved a condom from his wallet and joined her before she could finish pulling back the covers. Once he had sheathed himself, he lifted her onto the bed and followed her down, sliding his hips between her thighs and pushing inside her. Her body forgot how out of practice she was. She was tight for a few moments, but he held himself still until she relaxed and stretched to accommodate him. Then she was the one who reached between them and urged him to complete her. She felt more female, more alive than she had in years. She wanted this. She wanted him. Beneath Burke's hands, she felt beautiful, sexy. He coaxed her body to a peak and she crashed over, holding him in her arms and deep inside her as he crested the same wave and found his release. His guttural moan of satisfaction was as heady as any sweet nothing he could have whispered in her ear.

Sometime later, after Burke had brought her a damp washcloth and closed the door to keep the dogs from joining them, Hazel sank back onto her pillow and exhaled a deeply contented sigh. They were lying on their backs, side by side, their naked bodies still cooling from the intense lovemaking they'd shared.

Burke reached for her hand between them. "You okay?"

She laced her fingers together with his. "I'd like to say it's like riding a bicycle. But…it was never like that before. I can't feel my bones. I feel glorious." She turned her head to see him on the pillow beside hers and felt a tug of something precious and fragile in her heart. "You?"

He rolled onto his side, facing her. "You were worth the wait."

Could there be any more doubt that she loved this man? That she needed him? He was good for her ego. Good for her body. Good for her, period.

But what exactly was he getting out of this relationship besides some seriously hot benefits and…vet care for his K-9 team?

"Jedediah…"

"Dr. Cooper." When he leaned in to kiss her again, his stomach growled, saving her from asking the question she needed to. Maybe those seriously hot benefits were enough for him right now.

Laughing against his kiss, she patted his stomach. His muscles jumped beneath the simple touch, and she quickly pulled her hand away from the temptation to repeat what they'd just shared. "We'd better take care of a few other priorities."

Seizing the opportunity to end the encounter on a positive note instead of dragging the mood down with her worries again, she scrambled off the bed and opened the closet door to pull out the T-shirt and pajama pants hanging on a hook there. "We forgot dinner. We should eat before we fall asleep from exhaustion."

Avoiding the questioning look on his face, Hazel quickly dressed, adding a pair of socks and a hoodie. Burke followed more slowly, swinging his legs off his side of the bed and watching her for several seconds before striding across the hall to the bathroom. "I'll take the dogs out one more time while you heat up some food."

Nearly two hours later, Hazel was lying on the bed, curled into a ball, trying to stay warm. Even her socks and hoodie and an afghan snugged around her couldn't chase away the thoughts that chilled her whole body. She heard Burke in the doorway behind her, identifying him by the soft rustle of his jeans and that spicy clean scent that was his alone.

She wasn't sure how long he hovered there, maybe just checking on her, or maybe trying to decide if he'd be welcome to rejoin her. She'd willingly taken their relationship far beyond the friendship level this evening—it wouldn't be fair to backtrack from that closeness. Not to Burke. Not to either of them.

"I'm not asleep." Rolling over, she found him leaning against the door frame, cradling a mug of the decaf coffee she'd brewed earlier. "You don't have to watch over me 24-7."

He shook his head and came into the room. "Doesn't seem to be a habit I can break." The mattress shifted as he sat on the edge of the bed beside her. "You okay?" He set the mug on the bedside table and straightened the afghan around her. "After baring your soul—and a few other things—to me, you should be exhausted. You barely touched your dinner. And no ice cream, so I know something's wrong."

Ignoring his efforts to tuck her in, Hazel sat up to face him, hugging her knees to her chest. "Besides a stalker I can't identify who wants to blow me up?"

He didn't grin at her teasing. "Yeah. Besides that. You don't regret what happened between us, do you?"

"Other than feeling like I took advantage of your kindness?"

"Kindness?" Now he snickered a single laugh. He rested one hand on top of her knee. "I've been dreaming about making love to you for a couple of years now."

"But you kept your distance because I wanted you to."

"And then you didn't want me to. I don't think I could ever get my fill of you, Doc. But I do wonder about the timing. You've been under a lot of stress. And everything you told me—that was a major catharsis for you."

She couldn't argue that. "I needed to feel like me again for a little while. Like life is normal and people can want each other in a healthy way."

"I gather that's the healing part you wanted. But now you've had time to think." He smoothed her bangs across her forehead. "What's going on inside that head of yours? Help me understand."

Hazel captured his hand and clasped it between both of hers. It was strong and a little rough around the edges, but infinitely tender, just like the man himself. "Tonight…the devil man… He laughed at me, Jedediah. I was trying to keep him on the defensive, goad him into staying until KCPD got here. But I let it slip how scared I was, and that made him laugh. He said he'd take it as down payment on what I owe him."

His fingers flinched within her grasp, the only outward sign of his protective temper. "Like the jerk your ex hired. You said he laughed. Joked about the money. I'll need his name, too, by the way. In case he has a surviving relative or friend who might be interested in payback."

She nodded. "He's enjoying this. He's getting off on toying with me."

"He wants to get under your skin."

"He's succeeding." Hazel pulled her hands away to hug her knees again. "I've been completely honest with you—told you some things even my daughters have never heard. I know you need me to be strong. And I'd like to think that I am. But this relentless campaign—all the memories it has dredged up— it's wearing me down. It makes me question everything I say or think or do. The last time I was afraid for my life…"

Burke gathered her in his arms, afghan and all, and pulled her onto his lap. "The last time, you didn't have me. I've got your back."

For once, she was glad his patience had run out, and Hazel snuggled in, tucking her head beneath his chin. "Like Gunny will always have yours."

He nodded. "Trust your strength, Haze. Trust mine."

She did. But if there truly was going to be a future for them, she needed to know if she could hold up her end of the bargain, and be what he needed, too. "Can you trust me just as much? I know your ex-wife… You couldn't trust her."

"No. I couldn't," he said, falling back across the bed and pulling her on top of him, keeping her close. "You're a different class of lady. She never would have been so honest with me as you've been tonight. She never trusted that I could be there for her. If she wanted comfort, entertainment, a sounding board to dump on, she'd go find it. She still does. Hell. She'll call me if her current husband can't make things right for her."

"Not everyone is cut out to be the spouse of a man or woman in uniform."

"True. Shannon was sweet and perfect and everything I wanted in a high school sweetheart. But I became a soldier. And a cop. I saw the world—the good, the bad, the weird and the stuff I wish I could forget. I grew up. I don't know that she ever will." He shifted on the bed, angling them toward the pillows. "You're an adult, Haze. An equal. You've faced more adversity than she ever had to. And you dealt with it without compromising your integrity. You found your own strength. You asked for my help, but you didn't expect to be rescued."

Hazel changed topics, suspecting he'd rather talk about something a little less personal, even though she sensed there was more to Burke's past, just as there had been more to hers. "What did Justin mean when he said you and Gunny had saved him and his team?"

He probably recognized the diversion for what it was, judging by the squeeze of her hand between them. "Usually, a K-9 unit is deployed along with the bomb squad when there's a call. We clear the building, make sure there are no secondary explosives planted in the area."

"Have you ever found secondary explosives?"

"Yes."

His simple answer probably downplayed a good deal of the danger he and Gunny had faced helping their brothers in blue and protecting the city.

"You take care of a lot of people, don't you?" she observed. "I don't want to be another burden to—"

"Do not finish that sentence." A warm, callused finger pressed against her lips. "I'm here by choice, not because it's my job. Not because of the crazy good sex we had."

"Will you stay with me?" she asked.

"I thought that was the plan." He pointed to the doorway. "I'll be right out there. Gunny's already sacked out."

"No. Will you stay *here*?" She patted the bed beside her. "To sleep. Is that asking too much of you and your patience?"

He rolled onto his side, pulling her into his chest. "Me holding you? I think I can manage."

"You smell good," she murmured on a drowsy sigh against his soft cotton T-shirt. "Justin has no business calling you *old man*. You're a man, period. Warm.

Solid. One hell of a kisser…among other talents. I love touching you. You feel good."

"Do I feel safe?"

She nodded.

He pressed a kiss to her forehead. "Then close your eyes, Doc."

She did. Minutes later, physically and emotionally spent but snug in the shelter of Burke's embrace, she fell into an exhausted sleep.

Chapter Twelve

With his gun on the nightstand beside him, and Gunny dozing by the door, Burke finally dropped his guard long enough to fall into a deep, contented sleep. The dogs would alert him long before any threat reached him. He could use a solid seven or eight hours to rebuild his stamina after burning the candle at both ends to keep an eye on Hazel, track down leads on her stalker and work his own shift duties at the training center.

And then there were the physical demands of that frantic, powerful lovemaking session with Hazel. A blissful sense of peace spilled over from his conscious thoughts and filled his dreams.

He was the only man Hazel wanted. He was certain of it. More certain than he'd ever been with his own wife all those years ago. He reveled in the knowledge that Hazel wanted him enough to demand a mutual seduction, needed him enough to trust him with her secrets. She trusted him with her body, her life. And even though he wondered if she recognized it herself, she trusted him with her heart.

An annoying buzz tried to pull him from his sweet dreams, and he shifted in his sleep. Like a man half his age, he ached to be with her again already, to feel her grasping at him, squeezing around him, calling out his name. Although the images were vague, the sensations were as real as the heat cocooning his body, opening every pore, firing up the blood coursing through his veins. He'd dreamed of Hazel before, but not as vividly as this. Laugh by laugh, conversation by conversation, he'd fallen a little more in love with Hazel Cooper every day. Now he wanted to hold on to the closeness he and the curvy vet had finally shared. He had someone in his life again after all this time. He'd waited for it to be right—he'd waited for her. Now he had more than a friend, more than a fantasy dutifully hidden away in his deepest dreams. He had a partner. He'd be safe with her. He could be who he needed to be, do what he needed to do, and never worry that she couldn't understand the call to duty that drove him. She possessed that same sense of duty—to her children, her patients. She wouldn't leave him for something easier, someone immediately available, and he wouldn't leave her. This had been his vision for so long. He knew where he wanted this relationship to go, what he wanted to ask her.

He'd take her to dinner. No, take her to the dog park. He could tie the ring to Gunny's harness and...

The incessant buzzing ruined the future he was planning with her. He opened his eyes to the darkness. As awareness rapidly pinged through his brain, Burke remembered he was in Hazel's bedroom. He was half-aroused from a soft thigh wedged between his legs, and he was suffused with heat. He didn't remember burrowing beneath the covers, and he realized now that he hadn't. Not only was Hazel snuggled in like a blanket with her omnipresent afghan, the dogs had joined them on the bed.

And a phone was ringing.

"Damn." He wasn't on duty for another thirty-two hours. Something major must be playing out somewhere in the city for an alert to reach out to off-duty personnel. He patted the back pocket of his jeans. "Where's my phone?"

Hazel was awake, too. She crawled to the nightstand on her side. "It's mine," she murmured, lifting Cleo out of the way.

Burke pushed Gunny off his feet and ordered him to the floor. "What time is it?"

"Too early for a phone call." She fumbled for her phone long enough that he reached up to turn on the lamp beside him. "Make that too late. I'm not the emergency vet on call tonight, so it must be one of my own patients… Oh, hell." She hit the answer button and sat bolt upright. "Ashley?"

"Mom!"

He heard the faint cry of panic over the phone and sat up with Hazel, instantly on alert. He braced his arm behind her back and leaned in. "Put it on speaker."

"Sweetheart, what's wrong?" Tension radiated through Hazel's body.

Ashley was panting or sobbing or both. "I need you

to come get me. My car is still at the clinic. I'd call Polly, but I don't think it's safe for her to come here."

The distinct sound of glass breaking made Hazel jump. "What was that? Where are you? Are you all right?"

Men swearing and cheering in the background was not a good sign.

Burke clasped a hand over Hazel's shoulder and spoke into the phone. "Ashley, where are you? What's happening?"

"Sergeant Burke?"

No time to explain why he was on her mother's phone at one in the morning. "Answers, Ash."

Like most people, she responded to his calm, succinct tone. "Joe brought me to this biker bar—Sin City. I could tell this place was a dive even before I saw the drunk passed out at one of the tables. He said these are his friends. Only, somebody did something to someone's bike—I'm not sure what happened. This guy joked that I could pay for the damage." She squealed a split second before he heard chairs knocking over. All sure signs that a fight had broken out. "He wasn't talking about money."

Hazel shivered. "Oh, my God."

"That's when Joe punched him. Oh!" She must have dodged a falling man or flying debris. "Can you come?"

"I know the place." Burke was already out of bed, tucking in his T-shirt and reaching for his belt with his badge and gun. He wasn't taking the time to change into his uniform. "Can you get to the women's restroom and lock yourself in? Or get behind the bar and duck down? It's solid."

"The fight's in here." Ashley was breathing fast, either from physical exertion or fear. "Aren't I safer outside?"

"Not in that part of town."

Hazel had scrambled off the bed, too, circling around to keep the phone close to him while he dressed. "Where's Joe now?" she asked.

"In the parking lot maybe? That's where the argument started. It's like gangs taking sides. I came inside to report it. The bartender called the police."

"Good. They'll be there any minute. It's not far from HQ. Tell them you're a friend of mine. I'm on my way." Burke headed across the hall to the bathroom, where he'd left his bag, to retrieve socks and a pullover. Hazel was right by his side. "Can you get someplace safe?"

Ashley considered her options, then started moving. "This place is long and skinny—I don't think I can get all the way to the bathroom in the back. I'm heading behind the bar now."

A deeper, quieter voice sounded closer than the chaos at the bar. *"Come with me, miss."*

"Who's that?" Burke asked.

"I don't know..." Something crashed. There was a grunt of pain. "Oh! Stop that! Are you okay?"

"Sweetie, who are you talking to?" Hazel demanded, handing Burke his second boot to tie on.

"A man. I don't know," Ashley answered. "An old guy who was sitting at the bar. Another guy just clocked him with his elbow taking a swing at some-one else."

"Come with me." There was a scuffling sound and a choice insult for some *old man* before the noises of the fight faded.

Ashley spoke again. *"Are you okay? I have some medical training. Here. Put a towel on it. I'll get some ice."*

Then the deep, breathy voice came back within hearing range. *"I can take you somewhere. Home? A friend's house? Coffee shop? Anywhere but here, right?"* His laughter faded into a wheezing cough.

"Do not leave with anybody," Burke ordered, strid-ing toward the front door to retrieve Gunny's har-ness. Hazel hurried along beside him. "I'm on my way to get you."

"We're on our way. Be safe, sweetie." Hazel dis-connected the call.

Burke glanced down at her pajamas and stock-inged feet. "I'm leaving in two minutes. As soon as I get Gunny geared up."

She stepped into her discarded shoes beside the door and grabbed her jacket. "No need to wait."

No way was Hazel sitting locked inside Burke's truck while he waded through this mess of drunks with leather and attitude to find her daughter. But a stern warning about not needing the distraction of keep-ing an eye on her when he needed to watch his own back and rescue Ashley made enough sense that she had agreed to wait just outside his truck, where she could watch everything from across the street and pace away her fears. How had her daughter gotten stuck in the middle of all this mess?

Hazel had helped with natural disaster recovery scenes that didn't have this many police cars and uniformed officers on-site. Sin City certainly lived up to its name as a bar where no one with any good sense belonged. Apparently, Joe Sciarra's argument had triggered the rivalry between two motorcycle clubs. And Ashley had been caught in the middle of it all while her soon-to-be-*ex* boyfriend, Hazel hoped, had sided with his bros instead of getting her out of the melee.

The endless days of rain had finally stopped, but the wet pavement reflected the swirling patterns of red and blue lights and piercing fog lamps from the silent police cruisers, distorting the darting figures of innocent patrons hurrying to escape the police presence and bloodied combatants trying to get in one last lick before they were lined up against the wall or ordered to the ground and handcuffed. Like wraiths sliding in and out of the darkness, officers, brawlers and bystanders alike were being shuffled to various locations—to one of the ambulances that were here to treat a variety of minor injuries, to the parking lot to drive or ride away, or to one of the waiting black-and-white police vehicles.

She huffed out a sigh of relief when Burke appeared in the doorway, with his arm around Ashley's shoulders, her daughter clutched protectively by his side. "Ashley!"

Even as she danced inside her shoes, eager to run to her daughter but mindful of Burke's warning to keep a safe distance, Hazel felt her chin angling up with pride at the sight of the crowd parting for Burke, Ashley and Gunny. The man could sure clear a path. He oozed the sort of authority that made his coworkers respect him and the perps shy out of his way. He should have had children, she thought, sadly— he'd make a fabulous father. Protector. Father figure. Friend. Lover. And he was hers. All hers. If she was brave enough to claim him.

When she couldn't wait another second to know that her daughter was safe, and the man she loved was responsible for that gift, Hazel darted across the street. "Ashley!"

"Mom!" Her older daughter pulled away from Burke and fell into Hazel's tight hug.

"I'm so glad you're okay. *Are* you okay?" She pulled back to frame Ashley's face in her hands. Flushed cheeks, a little pale, but no sign of injury or tears.

"I'm fine, Mom." Ashley's smile confirmed that fact. "I had the daylights scared out of me. But I never was so happy to see Burke walking into that bar."

"I know the feeling." Hazel lifted her gaze to the man waiting patiently beside them. She palmed his grizzled cheek, stretched up on tiptoe and planted a firm kiss square on his mouth. "Thank you," she whispered, then kissed him again, lingering as his lips clung to hers. "Thank you."

When she sank back to her heels, heat was simmering in Burke's dark eyes and her daughter was grinning from ear to ear. "Um, what's happening here?" Ashley pointed back and forth between her and Burke. "And are you wearing your pajamas under your coat?"

"Oh, sweetie," Hazel began. "So much has happened—"

"Hold that thought." Ashley's smile vanished and heat flooded her cheeks as her gaze focused on a point beyond Burke. "I need to have a conversation."

"Whoa." When Burke reached out to stop her from charging back into the chaos, Hazel grabbed his arm and silently asked him to stay put.

She'd seen a black-haired man with too many tattoos being handcuffed and led to the back seat of a police cruiser, too. "Let her go."

"Not by herself." Burke clasped Hazel's hand and pulled her into step beside him. With a nod to the officer who initially warned Ashley to stay back, Burke stopped a few feet away, allowing the meeting with Joe Sciarra to happen, but not interfering.

Joe's left eye was bruised and puffy, and a raspberry had been scraped across his cheek. But Ashley wasn't interested in him being hurt. Hazel's girl was fired up. "They said you started the fight. You brought me here, looking to trade punches with Bigfoot over there?"

"Hey!" The overbuilt man's protest was cut short by the petite uniformed officer palming his head and guiding him into the back of her police cruiser.

Ashley waited for an answer from the man she'd

been seeing. "It's nothing personal. I owed a favor and Digger needed the cash. You were fun enough to make the deal worthwhile."

"What deal? With who?" Ashley demanded.

"It was a win-win situation, baby." He winked. "You know you liked hangin' with a bad boy."

"What are you talking about? What's going on?"

Joe scanned the street and parking lot before nodding toward the guy in a baggy, long jacket and jeans sneaking down the sidewalk. "Ask *him*."

The notion of something familiar, something off, jolted through Hazel as she watched the man with the graying blond ponytail and shaggy beard walking away. She released Burke's hand and took a step toward the man. Then another. And another. Fury blazed white-hot, clearing her thoughts, and she started running.

"Haze!" A strong hand clamped over her arm, stopping her. "What is it with you Cooper women?" Burke challenged. "I'm trying to get you away from the danger. Where are you going?"

"That man. I know him." She patted Burke's chest, willing him to see the urgency in catching up with the man before he disappeared. "At Saint Luke's Hospital. He's one of the homeless men Polly works with."

Ashley appeared beside her, studying the man as he glanced behind him and quickened his pace. "He tried to break up the fight. Help me get away. But he got hurt. He took a pretty good punch. Cut his lip and bloodied his nose. They were too out of control in there for him to do much good. But I should thank him for trying."

The man turned around and Hazel cursed. Even from a distance, through the night's distorted lights, she knew him. The man looked straight at her, then spun away, quickly disappearing into an alley. "Put Ashley in your truck."

Burke's hold tightened. "You're not following some guy down a dark alley in the middle of the night."

"Then come with me." She tugged on Burke's grip. "Aaron!"

He released her. "As in Aaron Cooper?"

"Dad?" Ashley echoed.

Burke waved an officer over to his truck and told the young man to keep an eye on Ashley. He and Gunny quickly caught up with Hazel in the alley. She halted beside a pile of trash cans and garbage bags that smelled like a used litter box. The setting was fitting for this reunion.

The man turned beneath the light from the side entrance to a neighboring building. The face was a little more weathered from sun and age, but she knew those blue eyes. Once upon a time she'd loved them. Later, they'd haunted her nightmares.

"What the hell are you doing here, Aaron?"

His shaggy appearance was a far cry from the tailored suit-and-tie up-and-comer she'd once loved. "Hazel. How's it goin', babe?"

"Don't *babe* me. This is no coincidence. What are you doing at Sin City on this particular night?"

"I was trying to save my little girl."

She rolled her eyes to the starry sky and curbed her tongue before she spoke again. "You were at the hospital with Polly, too, weren't you? Are you really homeless?"

He shrugged. "I got a place." His gaze drifted over her shoulder to the man standing behind her. "Nothing fancy like the home where we used to live."

"It was a fairy-tale facade you created, not a home. Not at the end." She might have known the truth, but she had refused to accept her marriage was a sham and her husband couldn't be trusted until the night Aaron's friend had tried to kill her. Her love and loyalty had meant nothing to him. His attempt to reminisce and claim there was a bond they still shared meant nothing to her now. "You've insinuated yourself into Polly's life, haven't you?"

"She and I are friends."

"Friends?"

"She's a kindhearted girl." He smiled. "Like you used to be."

"Does she know who you are?"

"She knows me as Russell, an Army vet who's having a hard time adjusting to life outside." She hadn't expected him to admit his deception. The old Aaron would have stuck with the lie to the very end— unless a different lie could save him. "That's not so far from the truth. I'm struggling to adjust to life away from Jeff City. Making the right friends. Finding a decent job. Not being judged."

"Why would someone judge you? A convicted

felon." Sarcasm rolled out with a sharp bite that should have embarrassed her.

"Hell, Hazel, she didn't even recognize me. She doesn't remember me at all."

"You were in prison, not the military. You were there because of the choices you made. You could have done the right thing and admitted your guilt and paid back what you stole. You'd have been out a decade sooner and had a lot of years knowing your daughters."

He could justify any action that benefited himself. "If I can't be their father, then I want to know them however I can."

"By stalking them? Do you know how frightening that is? How did you know Ashley was on a date here tonight? How did you know a fight would…" She shook her head, no longer regretting the sarcasm. "What con are you running this time?"

"I'm not hurting them. I just want to be a part of their lives."

The moment he took a step toward her, she felt a strong hand settle at the small of her back. Burke believed that she could handle this confrontation with her ex, but he was letting both her and Aaron know that he was there if she needed him. Sizing up the big man with the big dog, Aaron retreated half a step.

"Polly was easy. My parole officer put me onto Saint Luke's program to help the homeless and those who can't afford health care. I knew it was her the moment I saw her. She looks just like you when we met." He frowned. "Except for the hair. What'd you do to yours?"

Irrelevant. "And Ashley?"

He pulled back the front of his jacket and thrust his hands into his pockets. For a split second she felt tension stiffen Burke's fingers at her back. Had he expected to see a weapon? Wires attached to a bomb trigger? The tension gradually eased as Aaron continued. "I know Joe Sciarra from inside. Gave him some financial advice so he had a nest egg waiting for him when he got out."

"I'm not even going to ask if that advice was legal or not. You got a guy who owed you a favor to charm your daughter and set her up in a situation where she could have been hurt?"

"He wasn't supposed to hurt Ash. Just scare her. Then I could come in and save the day. Make her grateful to me. I guess it got out of hand."

She wanted to walk over and slap his face for manipulating their children like that. But that would involve touching him, and that thought was about as abhorrent as the idea that no one she loved was safe from his machinations. "How dare you put our daughter in danger for your selfish whims. I guess some habits you'll never break."

"I'm sorry, babe, but your damn restraining orders force me to be resourceful."

Hazel shook her head at the utter waste of a lifetime. "I think of all the good things you could have done with that brain of yours. How much you could have accomplished. If you'd used your people skills to help someone besides yourself—"

"Could've, would've, should've, huh?"

She almost felt sorry for the regret that momentarily aged his expression. *Momentarily.*

"Look, I need to talk to you about something," he continued. "I've been worried about you."

"I'm not your concern."

"Right. That's what New Boyfriend is for." He spared a condescending glance up at Burke, then focused on her again. "Then let's say I'm worried about the girls. That's why I wanted to get close to them. I think someone is after me. You know? Fifteen years behind bars isn't enough satisfaction for a lot of people—"

"I can't do this tonight, Aaron. I need to take care of Ashley." She turned to walk away. She'd wanted to confirm that Aaron had insinuated his way into their lives again and to put him on notice that she wouldn't tolerate his games anymore. She wasn't hanging around to make nice or assuage his conscience.

"Gunny, *fuss*," Burke ordered, falling in behind her.

But Aaron had never liked her asserting herself. "This guy has shown up every place I've been. At Saint Luke's. Your clinic—"

Hazel whirled around. "You've been to my clinic?"

"I watch from the strip mall across the street sometimes. Getting a look at what I've lost. You built a nice place for yourself." He grinned smugly at Burke. "Don't worry, I keep my hundred yards away from her. You can't arrest me for parking my car in a public lot."

Aaron had been close by this whole time? "I knew someone was watching me, but I thought… You need to stop."

"I think he's following me. Or he's following the girls…" He swallowed a curse. Was he losing his temper with her? "While you're shacking up with your new boyfriend here, I've been keeping an eye on Ash and Polly. I tried to tell you something was hinky, but you won't take my calls."

"Why would I believe anything you tell me?"

His anger exploded. "I have the right to protect my own children! If you're putting them in danger—"

"That's rich, coming from you."

"Time out." Burke silenced them both. "Priorities, Haze." He moved up beside her, then edged himself closer to Aaron. "Tell me about the man you've seen following Hazel and the girls."

"I don't have to tell New Boyfriend anything. Even if he does wear a badge. Hell, especially if he wears a badge."

"If you really want to man up and protect your children," Burke taunted, "talk to me." Hazel heard the threat in his voice. "The guy you've seen has been playing with bombs."

"Bombs?" Aaron frowned, looking honestly taken aback by the grim statement. "Polly's car? He did that?"

Burke gave a sharp nod. "He's been to the clinic and Hazel's building—with explosives and bomb parts both times. He probably knows where your daughters live, too. I need to find him before he pushes the button that could take out your entire family and a bunch of innocent bystanders."

"Bombs?" Aaron's thoughts wandered away.

"Do you know this guy?" Burke prodded.

"Not really." Aaron shrugged. "But I used to get anonymous letters in prison from some guy who said he was going to be waiting on the outside for me—to blow me up the way I blew up his life."

A chill skittered down Hazel's spine. "Oh, my God."

"Do you still have a client list of the people you cheated?" Burke asked.

When his only response was a resentful glare, Hazel answered. "It's probably in the archives at the DA's office. They were all listed as victims in the lawsuit."

Burke nodded, pulling his phone from his jeans. "It's a long shot, but let me make a few calls. I'll wake somebody up to see if the prison has any record of who sent those letters, and cross-match it with names from the DA's office. Maybe one of your clients has a job with access to explosives. At the very least, we can determine if the letters came from the same person. Here." He handed Gunny's lead to Hazel. "You know most of the commands. Use him if you need to." He gave Aaron a pointed look before he walked off a few steps to use his phone.

The moment they were superficially alone, Aaron grew defensive. "If this guy was one of my clients, he can't blame me for losing his money. There's always a risk with investments. Things happen."

Things happen. Like the man you entrusted your money to might devise a scheme to funnel all your profits into his own offshore bank account, all while selling a bill of goods that would make you want to keep paying him more money.

"You still don't understand that your actions have repercussions that affect your entire family. We're still paying the price for your greed. You may not be directly involved in what's happening to us now, but if this guy was one of your investors, you're responsible."

"The years have been good to you, babe." His wistful tone had no effect on her. "But I miss your long hair."

"It was too much work. *You* were too much work."

"I was a rich man, Hazel. The four of us would be sitting pretty right now if you'd have just kept your mouth shut." When he reached out to touch her hair, Hazel recoiled.

"Gunny?" The big dog growled beside her. Aaron wisely stepped back with hands up in surrender. *"Sitz."* The big shepherd plopped down into a sit position beside her.

"You've changed."

"You haven't." Neither had the threat surrounding her. "Please. Tell me anything you can about the man you saw. The only times I've gotten close enough to identify him, it was dark, and he was wearing a mask."

Finally, either for his daughters or for her or to avoid dealing with Gunny, Aaron nodded. "The guy I saw is about my height. More of a paunch—I did a lot of working out in prison. The loose clothes are part of my disguise." Unimpressed with his sales pitch, she rubbed the top of Gunny's head and waited for him to continue. "He's a white guy. Does manual labor, I'm guessing. Like a mechanic, maybe. He wears a uniform under that hoodie. His hands were dirty. White hair. I never got a good look at his face."

Never missing an important clue, Burke rejoined the conversation. "Anything else? Did you see what he drives?"

Aaron shook his head. "He was always on foot when I saw him." He snapped his fingers as an idea hit. "Tobacco. I've seen him spit a chaw more than once."

A chaw of tobacco. Why did that seem familiar? Did she know anyone who chewed? Was there something behind the devil man's mask she could identify?

While the wheels turned inside her head, looking for answers, Burke's hand settled at her back again. "You can walk away this time, Cooper. But if you violate your restraining order and come near any of these women again, I'll be there."

Aaron's glare was less pronounced this time. Without thanking Burke for giving him a break, Aaron turned to Hazel. "Would you talk to the girls and see if they'd be interested in getting to know me? Unless you've poisoned them against me."

"I'll ask them. No guarantees. It will be their

Julie Miller   233

choice. And frankly, with the lies you've been telling, you're not off to a great start. You'll have to live with whatever they decide. I won't let you hurt them again."

"Thanks." He turned and headed head down the alley toward the next cross street.

"And, Aaron?" He turned to hear her out. "If you really want a relationship with them—no games, no lies. Be patient. Be real." Like this man beside her. She clasped Burke's hand and headed out of the alley. "I want to see my daughter now."

BURKE ADJUSTED HIS wraparound sunglasses on the bridge of his nose as he drove back into the city after spending several hours at the K-9 training center. It felt prophetic to feel the sun warming his skin through the windshield again. After so many days of one rainstorm after another, the October sun felt more like the beginning of a new page in his life instead of the last hurrah of summer.

It had been a long night with little sleep, but he felt energized by anticipation rather than fatigued. His life was changing, and he was ready for it. His patience with Hazel had paid off. They were a thing now—in a relationship. And once he figured out who was behind all the threats and put the crud behind bars, he intended to make that relationship permanent. He ignored his goofy grin reflected in the mirror. There were some things even his patience couldn't wait for.

After leaving the Sin City bar in KCPD's capable hands, they'd driven straight to Ashley and Polly's apartment, where the three Cooper women shared a laughing, tearful "yell me everything that happened" reunion that included several warm hugs for him and thank-you bites of cheese for Gunny. At his insistence, to streamline their security and for their mother's peace of mind, Ashley and Polly packed up their bags, and he loaded them into his truck. Although he was a little amazed at the toiletries-to-clothing ratio each young woman stuffed into her small suitcase, like their mother, they'd been quick and efficient. Then he'd dismissed Officer Cho and driven them all back to Hazel's condo, where she served the girls hot chocolate, encouraged them to talk as late as they wanted to and succinctly announced that he would be sleeping in her room. With her. If the girls had any objections to those arrangements, they could talk about it in the morning.

He didn't know whether to laugh or be nervous when breakfast that morning had been eerily quiet.

Garrett Cho had stopped by to pick up Polly and drive her to class at Saint Luke's, and Burke struggled with an unfamiliar urge to take the younger man aside and find out more about his background and his interest in Polly. Then he'd driven Hazel and Ashley to work, and gone to his office at the K-9 training center to follow up on last night's phone calls regarding the leads they'd gotten from Hazel's ex. Some of the leads were paying off as Detectives Bellamy and Cartwright ran down the short list of potential suspects from the list of Aaron Cooper's swindle victims. If any of those names connected to explosives, and crossed paths with Hazel's world, then chances were they had their man. Besides, the Cooper women were babying Gunny enough that he wanted to run the dog through his paces to make sure he remembered he was a trained police officer and not a spoiled house pet.

His time with Hazel and her daughters was crazy, chaotic and full of love. It was the life he wanted. He glanced at the dog panting behind him in the rearview mirror. "You okay with that, partner? You know you're still my number one guy, right?"

Gunny whined in response to being talked to. Burke decided to interpret the dog's excitement as an agreement. But his own smile quickly faded as his phone on the dash lit up with a call from his ex, Shannon. Better deal with this issue, too, if he wanted that life with Hazel.

He punched the answer button and immediately put it on speaker. "Sergeant Burke here."

"You know it's me, Jed." Her sultry voice held a little of that poor-me, damsel-in-distress tone. "Is this a good time to talk?"

With her? Never. But there were some things they needed to settle, once and for all. "I know you went to see Dr. Cooper. Were you checking out the competition?" He flicked his signal to shift into the passing lane. "FYI? There is no competition."

"So you two are serious about each other?"

"Yes."

Judging by that huff of breath, it wasn't the answer she wanted to hear. "Do you love her?"

"I do."

"You and I can never...?"

"No." His answer was gentle but as firm as he could make it. "Go home, Shannon. Talk to Bill and work things out. He loves you."

Discussion done, as far as he was concerned. He disconnected the call and breathed a sigh of relief. He was one step closer to the future he wanted.

He was cruising to a stop when his radio flared to life. "Delta K-9 one, please respond." The dispatcher relayed a call to bomb squad personnel summoning him to a Bravo Tango at a Front Street address.

Bravo Tango.

Bomb threat.

Burke swore. He turned on the siren and lights and stomped on the accelerator. He barely heard the dispatcher's apology about calling him in on his day off, or her explanation about the other bomb detection dog being out on another call. He punched in Hazel's number on the phone. It went straight to voice mail.

He picked up his radio. "Delta K-9 one—10-4." He answered that he was responding to the call and raced through the red light.

He knew that address.

Hazel's clinic.

Chapter Thirteen

"What the hell are you still doing in here?"

Six feet plus of angry Jedediah Burke coming through the swinging door of her operating room, armed and dressed in full protective gear, was a scary thing to behold.

Hazel already knew the clock was ticking; she didn't need him startling her like that. "I'm working as fast as I can. I was in the middle of surgery. I had to at least close her up before I could move her." She tied off another suture in the abdomen of the skinny cattle dog mix. "I told everyone to leave and put Todd in charge of evacuating all the animals."

"Nobody's here but you and that dog. Part of our sweep means getting all personnel off the premises before we even search for explosives." He and Gunny circled to the opposite side of the table. "What can I do to help?"

"Get out of my light, for one." She waved him back a step and concentrated on finishing up as quickly, if not as thoroughly, as she normally did. He glanced around the small surgery room, then put Gunny to work searching, making sure this room, at least, hadn't been rigged to explode. "Is it as bad as those sirens out there make it sound?"

"This area's clear," Burke replied, though it didn't help her feel relieved. "How much longer?"

"Todd and I were in the middle of this operation when Ashley told me a client found a brown paper package in the men's room." The picture Ashley had shown her had looked frighteningly familiar. "It's just like the one the devil man had."

"There's another one at the front door. Gunny hit on it."

Her hand shook and she nearly dropped her needle. "There's more than one?"

He moved in beside her, resting his hand on her shoulder. "Easy, Doc. You got this. But work a little faster."

Gunny suddenly jumped to his feet, his sharp ears pricked toward the door. When Burke pushed the door open slightly to check out the canine alarm, she heard the snuffling and whining, too. "Do I hear a dog in the back? Where's Todd?"

"KCPD's set up a perimeter. Nobody is allowed back in the building."

"We have to get him." He gave her a pointed look. One. More. Stitch. "I can't leave my patients…" When she saw that he was about to argue, she shook her head. "You wouldn't leave Gunny behind."

He gave her a curt nod. "I'll get whoever is in the kennel. Finish up."

Moments later, he was back with Shadow, the big Lab, in his arms. "We're all clear. Let's go."

Hazel frowned, remembering something important about the dog on the operating table. Athena had perked up with a little food and fluids, and was fit enough to be spayed.

"What is it?"

"Tobacco."

"What?"

Hazel shook off the unfinished thought. This wasn't the time to be solving mysteries. "Nothing. Go. I just have to give her an injection to wake her up. I'll be right behind you."

"Make sure you are."

He pushed through the swinging steel door. Seconds later, she heard the back door opening and closing. She gave the injection, made sure she had a heartbeat and breath sounds, then disconnected the dog from the oxygen mask and IV. The back door closed again. Burke wouldn't let her be at risk for very long. She wrapped a blanket around the groggy canine and lifted her in her arms. "We're coming."

It took a split second for the odd sound to register. The door hadn't opened and closed a second time.

Someone had locked it.

But she was already pushing through the swinging metal door out of the surgery room. "Burke?"

She pulled up short.

The devil man.

"Ticktock, Dr. Coop." He held up a triggering device, like the one he'd showed her that night outside her building, and laughed. His thumb rested on the button. "Is it on or off? How long do we have?"

She shrank back against the metal door. "How did you get in here?"

"There are lots of places to hide away in all these little rooms. I just had to be patient." The man in the grotesque mask breathed heavily with excitement as he reached inside a different pocket and pulled out another trigger. He pressed that one. "On."

There was no countdown this time. The floor rocked beneath Hazel's feet and she stumbled as a deafening boom exploded at the front of the building. Some light debris from the ceiling floated down like snow, but more alarming were the pings and instant dents of a dozen tiny missiles hitting the other side of the metal door. That door had probably just saved her life. If she'd still been in the surgery room…

She pushed away from the wall where she'd fallen. "Are you crazy?"

Perhaps not the right thing to say. The devil man took a menacing step toward her and pulled out a third trigger to replace the one he'd just used to blow up the front of her building. He fisted it in front of her face and jammed the button with his thumb. "On! Now I'm finally getting what I want."

A heavy fist pounded on the exit door behind him. "Hazel!"

"Burke!"

"I'm not interested in company, Dr. Coop." The devil man opened the storage cabinet beside the back door and tossed piles of blankets and towels onto the floor so that she could see the bomb behind them.

"Get away from the building!" she warned, afraid that explosive was the one ticking now. "He's put a bomb by the back door!"

She heard cursing and running. The smells of sulfur and ash drifting through from the front of the clinic stung her nostrils.

She smelled something else, too.

Tobacco.

I've seen him spit a chaw more than once.

The disjointed pieces from so many sources finally fell into place. Hazel hugged the dog sleeping in her arms a little tighter and squared off against the man who'd made her life hell for too many long months. "Take off the mask, Wade."

He grunted, as if surprised to be recognized.

"Are you afraid to do this face-to-face? Afraid to show me the truth?"

He tapped one of the triggers. "Off." Then he pushed back his hood and tugged the plastic mask over his head. He grinned at her with his stained teeth. "Doesn't matter if you figured it out. I will destroy you. Just like your husband destroyed me."

"Can I at least get this dog to safety?"

"It's a stupid dog." He picked up the trigger again and frowned, as if he couldn't remember the sequence of the countdown.

Hazel did. But she wasn't going to tell him he'd turned the countdown off. The trigger in the other hand meant another device was already ticking toward detonation. "How can you care so little about life?" she asked, hoping to distract him from turning on the device again.

"Because I don't have one." The distraction didn't last for long. He pressed the button. "On. Aaron Cooper stole all my money. My life savings. My future. I lost my house, my truck. My friends called me an idiot for falling for his lies. I drank too much and finally lost a good job. I've been working on a road crew. I'm a trained engineer, and I've been working on a stinking road crew. That's where I found that dog you're holding."

"But your wife—"

"She left me. Earlier this year." Probably about the time the letters had started arriving. "She said she finally had enough of me being a loser."

"So you picked up the stray and blamed her, so the authorities would investigate her."

"Yeah. Sweet little bonus—causing her grief. If she'd been loyal to me, I might not have had to go to such drastic measures. But mostly I just needed a way to get to you. So I grabbed Athena and brought her in."

Because he couldn't get to Aaron. Maybe because no amount of punishment or atonement could make up for a ruined life.

"And the explosives? You picked them up on your job, too?"

"Where's your husband, Dr. Coop? Why isn't he

rotting in prison? Why isn't he dead? Where's my justice?"

"Aaron is not my husband. You're hurting the wrong person."

Her words didn't seem to be reaching him. She couldn't hear Burke outside anymore. She could barely hear her own thoughts over the fear pounding through her pulse. Wade had blocked her path to escape. He'd probably rigged this entire building to blow.

She *did* have a life. She had a career she loved. Two beautiful daughters. She hadn't told Jedediah that she loved him. "How many bombs are there?"

"I've left a present for you every time I came to your clinic, whenever I visited that scrawny dog. I'm gonna bring this place to the ground." He leaned in, running his tongue along his yellowed teeth. His eyes were rheumy with a serious lack of sleep—or madness. "You wanna see 'em?"

She backed away, glancing all around her, wondering if there was any safe place inside the clinic where she could barricade herself from the next explosion. "I believe you."

"Off." He laughed again, enjoying her distress. "Isn't it fun not knowing how many seconds you have left to live? It's kind of like not knowing how long you have until the next part of your life implodes." He took a step toward her, backing her down the hallway. "And the police have kindly cordoned off the area so it's just you and me and a countdown." Another step.

Was he pushing her toward something? Trapping her? "Your husband destroyed my life. Now I get to do the same to him. I want to destroy *everything*." He raised the trigger and clicked it. "On."

She heard the shattering noise of breaking glass from somewhere in the damaged part of the building. Hazel spun around.

"Gunny! *Fuss!*"

A streak of black and brown rushed past her. She nearly cried out with relief because she knew Burke wouldn't be far behind.

With a vicious snarl, Gunny leaped, chomping down on Wade Hanson's upstretched arm and swinging his legs around to pull the man down to the floor. Gunny twisted, his powerful jaws never losing their grip on the man's arm.

Wade was screaming as Burke stormed in.

"Gunny! *Aus!*" Burke gave the command for the dog to stop biting and ordered him back to his side. He pushed Hazel and Athena behind him and leveled his gun between both hands at the man on the floor. "Stay down!" While Hanson writhed on the floor, cradling his arm and complaining about stupid dogs and sharp teeth, Burke cuffed him and explained his miraculous appearance. "He locked the back door. I couldn't get in. When the front of the building blew, I thought the worst."

Hazel appreciated his fear, but there was no time to talk. "There are more bombs. He had two triggers in his hands. I don't know what they're attached to, but he said they're counting down."

"Then we're getting out of here." He hauled Wade to his feet and shouldered open the back door, shouting to the cops outside. "K-9 officer coming out! Gunny! *Fuss!*"

Running ahead, Gunny led the way to the fenced yard behind the building. Hazel hurried out next, carrying Athena.

Hanson laughed, even as Burke dragged him to safety. "Time's up."

Hazel spun around. "Burke!"

A wall of black protective gear snapped around her body and pushed her to the ground. Her clinic erupted with three thunderous booms. A storm of fire shot high into the air, while debris rained down on the mud and grass all around them.

It was nighttime again by the time Justin Grant, his bomb disposal team and the KCFD let Hazel back onto the premises again.

So much destruction. So much anger.

She and Burke had been treated for minor injuries and released while Wade Hanson was handcuffed to his hospital bed, being read his rights and the long list of charges leveled against him. She herself had cleaned and put a couple of stitches in a cut Gunny had suffered from flying shrapnel, while Todd had seen to Athena's recovery. All their patients had either been sent home or were being boarded at another animal hospital.

With the girls safely ensconced back at the condo, and Burke at precinct headquarters helping Justin fill out paperwork on the case, Hazel had returned to the clinic. Or what was left of it. Between the explosions, fire and all the water from KCFD's fire hoses, there was little left but the concrete slab and the frame of the kennel's back wall.

Sorting through the rubble for anything salvageable, Hazel was surprised that she didn't feel sad. She spotted a metal stool and waded through a puddle of standing water to set it upright. After drying the top with the sleeve of her jacket, she sat, scanning the place she had built all those years ago despite Aaron's wishes to the contrary.

She was happy—no, intensely relieved—that no one had gotten seriously hurt, not even one of her precious patients. This clinic represented her old life. And it had been razed to the ground. She would rebuild. With a more open floor plan with fewer places for crazed bombers with a vendetta to hide. She could upgrade the technology of the facility. She'd come back, stronger than ever.

When Gunny trotted up to her, she petted the dog and smiled. "Free health care for the rest of your life, young man. All the treats and toys you want, too."

"You're making my dog fat."

Hazel stood and smiled at the deep voice that sounded so tired, so sexy. "Did you finish up at work?"

Burke nodded. Somewhere along the way, he'd

showered and changed into a clean uniform. "We found all the bombs. Justin and his team neutralized them."

"You mean Gunny found them all," she teased.

"I mean this is finally over." Burke pushed aside a mangled examination table and joined her beside the stool. "Hanson has been arrested. Your ex is on notice and shouldn't cause you or the girls any more trouble."

"I wonder if Aaron will be called as a material witness by the DA's office. That would be an ironic twist. We'll see if anyone rams a car into him to keep him from testifying."

Burke chuckled. "You've got a wicked sense of humor, woman."

She rested a hand against his chest and smiled up at him. "What I've got is hope."

"Yeah?"

"You are the bravest man I know. The most loyal. The most caring. You put your heart on the line with me. Even when you didn't know how I felt yet."

His hands settled at her waist. "I knew how you felt, Doc. You just had to realize it."

She lost the smile, wanting him to understand how serious she was. "I love you, Jedediah Burke. I don't want to waste another day of my life believing that being safe is the same as being happy. I can have both. I deserve both. I'm safe with you. I always have been. I needed to break some old habits and finally believe it. And, God knows, you make me happy."

"You gonna marry me, then?" he asked. "I've been patient for a long time."

Nodding, she wound her arms around his neck and pulled him to her for a kiss. "You were worth the wait."

* * * * *

*Look for more stories featuring
the next generation of
Kansas City heroes by Julie Miller.
Coming Soon
Only from Harlequin Intrigue.*

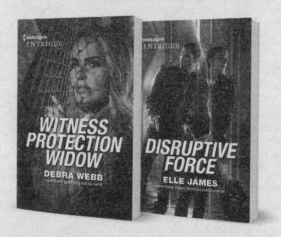

COMING NEXT MONTH FROM

H HARLEQUIN

INTRIGUE

Available August 18, 2020

#1947 CONARD COUNTY: HARD PROOF
Conard County: The Next Generation • by Rachel Lee
Former soldier and newbie deputy Candela "Candy" Serrano is assigned
as a liaison to Steve Hawks, the host of TV's *Ghostly Encounters*. Chasing
shadows isn't Candy's idea of police work, but soon some very real killings
start occuring around town...

#1948 HIS BRAND OF JUSTICE
Longview Ridge Ranch • by Delores Fossen
The only person who knows who killed Marshal Jack Slater's father is
Caroline Moser. But the Texas profiler has no memory of the murder, her
abduction...or Jack. Now in Jack's protective custody, Caroline must trust
her ex to help her recall her past before a murderer steals their future.

#1949 PROTECTIVE ORDER
A Badge of Honor Mystery • by Rita Herron
Reese Taggart's search for her sister's stalker lands her in Whistler, NC,
where she must win the trust of arson investigator Griff Maverick. But as the
pair close in on the criminal, can Griff stop Reese from using herself as bait?

#1950 BURIED SECRETS
Holding the Line • by Carol Ericson
To halt construction of a casino on Yaqui land, ranger Jolene Nighthawk
plants damning evidence. But she's caught by her ex, Border Patrol agent
Sam Cross. As Jolene and Sam investigate a series of deaths, they find that
their bodies may be the next ones hidden in Arizona sand.

#1951 LAST STAND SHERIFF
Winding Road Redemption • by Tyler Anne Snell
Soon after Remi Hudson tells Sheriff Declan Nash he's going to be a dad,
Remi becomes the target of repeated attacks. Declan will do anything to
keep her and their unborn baby safe, especially once he realizes the danger
is related to an unsolved case involving his family.

#1952 CAUGHT IN THE CROSSFIRE
Blackhawk Security • by Nichole Severn
When Kate Monroe's deceased husband suddenly appears, the profiler
can't believe her eyes. Declan Monroe has lost all of his memories, but
with a killer targeting Kate, the pair will have to work together to outwit the
Hunter...and find their way back to each other.

YOU CAN FIND MORE INFORMATION ON UPCOMING HARLEQUIN TITLES,
FREE EXCERPTS AND MORE AT HARLEQUIN.COM.

HICNM0820

SPECIAL EXCERPT FROM

✦ HARLEQUIN

INTRIGUE

While investigating a series of deaths in the Sonoran Desert, Border Patrol agent Sam Cross comes face-to-face with Jolene Nighthawk, the woman he once loved beyond all reason. Now, as the two join forces to get justice for the voiceless, old sparks reignite even as someone wants to make sure their reunion is cut short...

Keep reading for a sneak peek at Carol Ericson's Buried Secrets...

He grabbed his weapon and his wallet and marched out to his rental car. When did Border Patrol ever stop working? Especially when an agent didn't have anything better to do.

He pulled out of the motel parking lot and headed toward the highway. His headlights glimmered on the wet asphalt, but on either side of him, the dark desert lurked, keeping its secrets—just like a woman.

Grunting, he hit the steering wheel with the heel of his hand and cranked up the radio. Two days back, and the desert had already weaved its spell on him. He'd come to appreciate its mystical, magical aura when he lived here, but the memory had receded when he moved to San Diego. When he left Paradiso, he'd tried to put all those feelings aside—and failed.

When he saw the mile marker winking at him from the side of the road, he grabbed his cell phone and squinted at the directions. He should be seeing the entrance to an access road in about two miles. A few minutes later, he spotted the gap and turned into it, his tires kicking up sand and gravel.

His rental protested by shaking and jerking on the unpaved stretch of road. He gripped the wheel to steady it. "Hold on, baby."

A pair of headlights appeared in the distance, and he blinked. Did mirages show up at night? Who the hell would be out here?

His heart thumped against his chest. Someone up to no good.

As his car approached the vehicle—a truck by the look of it—he slowed to a crawl. The road couldn't accommodate the two of them passing each other. One of them would have to back into the sand, and a truck, probably with four-wheel drive, could do that a lot better than he could in this midsize with its four cylinders.

The truck jerked to a stop and started backing up at an angle. The driver recognized what Sam had already deduced. The truck would have to be the one to make way, but if this dude thought he'd be heading out of here free, clear and anonymous, he didn't realize he'd run headlong into a Border Patrol agent—uniformed or not.

Sam threw his car into Park and left the engine running as he scrambled from the front seat. The driver of the truck revved his engine. Did the guy think he was going to run him over? Take him out in the dead of night?

Sam flipped open his wallet to his ID and badge and rested his other hand on his weapon as he stalked up to the driver's side of the truck.

Holding his badge in front of him and rapping on the hood of the vehicle, he approached the window. "Border Patrol. What's your business out here?"

The window buzzed down, and a pair of luminous dark eyes caught him in their gaze. "Sam? Sam Cross?"

Sam gulped and his heart beat even faster than before as the beam of his flashlight played over the high cheekbones and full lips of the woman he'd loved beyond all reason.

Don't miss
Buried Secrets *by Carol Ericson,*
available September 2020 wherever
Harlequin Intrigue books and ebooks are sold.

Harlequin.com

Get 4 FREE REWARDS!

We'll send you 2 FREE Books plus 2 FREE Mystery Gifts.

Harlequin Intrigue books are action-packed stories that will keep you on the edge of your seat. Solve the crime and deliver justice at all costs.

FREE
Value Over
$20

YES! Please send me 2 FREE Harlequin Intrigue novels and my 2 FREE gifts (gifts are worth about $10 retail). After receiving them, if I don't wish to receive any more books, I can return the shipping statement marked "cancel." If I don't cancel, I will receive 6 brand-new novels every month and be billed just $4.99 each for the regular-print edition or $5.99 each for the larger-print edition in the U.S., or $5.74 each for the regular-print edition or $6.49 each for the larger-print edition in Canada. That's a savings of at least 12% off the cover price! It's quite a bargain! Shipping and handling is just 50¢ per book in the U.S. and $1.25 per book in Canada.* I understand that accepting the 2 free books and gifts places me under no obligation to buy anything. I can always return a shipment and cancel at any time. The free books and gifts are mine to keep no matter what I decide.

Choose one: ☐ **Harlequin Intrigue**
Regular-Print
(182/382 HDN GNXC)

☐ **Harlequin Intrigue**
Larger-Print
(199/399 HDN GNXC)

Name (please print)

Address   Apt. #

City   State/Province   Zip/Postal Code

Email: Please check this box ☐ if you would like to receive newsletters and promotional emails from Harlequin Enterprises ULC and its affiliates. You can unsubscribe anytime.

Mail to the **Reader Service:**
IN U.S.A.: P.O. Box 1341, Buffalo, NY 14240-8531
IN CANADA: P.O. Box 603, Fort Erie, Ontario L2A 5X3

Want to try 2 free books from another series? Call 1-800-873-8635 or visit www.ReaderService.com.

---

*Terms and prices subject to change without notice. Prices do not include sales taxes, which will be charged (if applicable) based on your state or country of residence. Canadian residents will be charged applicable taxes. Offer not valid in Quebec. This offer is limited to one order per household. Books received may not be as shown. Not valid for current subscribers to Harlequin Intrigue books. All orders subject to approval. Credit or debit balances in a customer's account(s) may be offset by any other outstanding balance owed by or to the customer. Please allow 4 to 6 weeks for delivery. Offer available while quantities last.

Your Privacy—Your information is being collected by Harlequin Enterprises ULC, operating as Reader Service. For a complete summary of the information we collect, how we use this information and to whom it is disclosed, please visit our privacy notice located at corporate.harlequin.com/privacy-notice. From time to time we may also exchange your personal information with reputable third parties. If you wish to opt out of this sharing of your personal information, please visit readerservice.com/consumerschoice or call 1-800-873-8635. **Notice to California Residents**—Under California law, you have specific rights to control and access your data. For more information on these rights and how to exercise them, visit corporate.harlequin.com/california-privacy.

HI20R2

SHARON SALA

**returns with the third book in her
Jigsaw Files series!**

He has nothing and everything to lose...

When a seventeen-year-old boy goes missing while camping with his buddies in the Chisos Mountains in Big Bend, the case is right up PI Charlie Dodge's alley. Charlie's reputation for finding missing people—especially missing kids—is unparalleled. Unfortunately, trouble seems to be equally good at finding him.

Charlie's still in the thick of it when bad news arrives regarding his wife, Annie, whose early-onset Alzheimer's is causing her to slip further and further away. The timing couldn't be worse. Thankfully, Charlie's ride-or-die assistant, Wyrick, has his back. But when Universal Theorem, the shadowy and elusive organization from Wyrick's past, escalates its deadly threats against her, it pushes both partners past their breaking points. Finding people is one thing; now Charlie will have to fight to hold on to everyone he holds dear.

Available now, from MIRA Books!

mira

Harlequin.com

MSS022

SPECIAL EXCERPT FROM

mira

*Read on for sneak peek at Sharon Sala's
new nail-biting thriller,*
Blind Faith.

One

The morning sun was hot on Tony Dawson's head, but his anger was hotter. This camping trip in Big Bend National Park was nothing but a setup—a betrayal—and by two people he had considered friends.

The drunken argument the three high school boys had last night had carried over into morning hangovers. They packed up camp in silence, and were nearing the junction that would take them back down to the Chisos Mountain Lodge where their overnight hike had begun.

Tony had nothing to say to either of them, which obviously wasn't what they'd expected, and as they neared the junction, both Randall Wells and Justin Young lengthened their strides to catch up to him.

"What are you going to do when you get back?" Randall asked.

Tony just kept walking.

Randall pushed him. "Hey! I'm talking to you!"

"Keep your damn hands off me. Not interested. Don't want to hear the sound of your lying voice. You said enough last night," Tony said.

"Are you going to keep seeing Trish? After all you found out?" Randall asked.

Tony fired back. "I had girlfriends back in California. I would assume they moved on when I left, because I did. So what if you dated Trish before I even knew her?"

"What about what Justin said?" Randall asked.

Tony stopped, then turned to face the both of them.

"You want the truth? I don't believe Justin. Why would I? You two lied about wanting to be my friend. You lied about this camping trip. It was a setup. You're both losers. Why would I believe two sore losers over my own instincts?"

Tony saw the rage spreading over Randall's face, but he wasn't expecting Randall to come at him.

Randall leaped toward him, swinging. Tony stepped to the side to dodge the blow, and when he did, the ground gave way beneath his feet. All of a sudden he was falling backward off the mountain, arms outstretched like Jesus on the cross, knowing he was going to die.

Two days later: Dallas, Texas

A Dallas traffic cop clocked the silver Mercedes at ninety-five miles per hour, and was just about to take off after it when his radar gun went dark, and then the car shot through a non-existent opening in the crazy morning traffic, before disappearing before his eyes.

"That did not just happen," he muttered, but just in case, radioed ahead for the next cop down the line to be on the lookout.

Wyrick wasn't concerned with the cop's confusion. She was already off the freeway and taking back streets to get to the office. She knew the cop had clocked her, but she had her own little system for blocking traffic radar, and she was in a bigger hurry than normal because she overslept—a rare occurrence.

Now, she just needed to get to the office before Charlie Dodge, or she'd never hear the end of it.

Finally, the office building came into view, and she sped through the last half mile without once tapping the brakes, skidded into her own parking place, and breathed a sigh of relief that Charlie's parking spot was still empty.

"That's what I'm talking about," she muttered, as she grabbed her things and got out on the run.

Within minutes of opening the office, she had coffee on, with the box of sweet rolls she'd picked up this morning plated beneath the glass dome in the coffee bar, and had both of their computers up and running.

She was going through the morning email when Charlie walked in, but she refused to look up. She knew what she looked like. She'd spent precious time this morning making sure she looked fierce, because she felt so damned wounded from the dreams.

"Bear claws under glass," she muttered. "Teenager missing in the Chisos Mountains in Big Bend. Are you interested?"

Charlie was used to Wyrick's outrageous fashion sense, and refused to be shocked by the black starbursts she'd painted around her eyes, the blood drop she'd painted at the corner of her mouth, the red leather cat suit, or the black knee-high boots she was wearing. But he was interested in the sugar crunch of bear claws, and kids who went missing.

"Yes, to both," he said, as he sauntered past. "Send me the stats on the missing kid, and get the parents in here for details."

"They're due here at 10:30."

He paused, then turned around, his eyes narrowing.

"Why do you even ask me what I want?"

"You're the boss," Wyrick said.

"I know that. I just didn't know you did," he mumbled.